# Moving In
## Moving In Series Book 1
### Written by Ron Ripley

D1738908

ISBN-13: 978-1523731329
ISBN-10: 152373132X

# Thank You and Bonus Novel!

I'd like to take a moment to thank you for your ongoing support. You make this all possible! To really show you my appreciation for purchasing this book, I've included a bonus scene at the end. **I'd also love to send you a full-length novel in 3 formats (MOBI, EPUB and PDF) absolutely free!**

Download your FREE novel in 3 formats, get FREE short stories, and receive future discounts by visiting www.ScareStreet.com/RonRipley

See you in the shadows,
Ron Ripley

# Moving In

## Chapter 1: The New House

Brian and Jenny stood on the porch of their new house and gazed at the stark New England farmland stretching out around them. The sun cast its last bit of light upon the yellowed grass, and a cold wind blew down from the north. There was a good chance of snow later in the evening. It would be the first of the season, the first in their new home, and Brian wasn't looking forward to it.

For all of his forty years Brian had lived in New Hampshire. Jenny, only three years younger, was a New Hampshire native too. But while Brian hated winter, Jenny had always enjoyed it.

Winter was only part of why Brian was anxious though. The rest of his anxiety had been a result of living in the city, the stress of his job. That, and the heart attack. All of it had forced the move out to the country. Brian had downsized his workload and was going to run his clients' security needs from a home office; once he had unpacked. But it didn't make him happy to be out of the city.

"What do you think?" Jenny asked, sliding her arm through his.

"About what?"

She looked up at him. "About this, all of this."

Brian smiled. "It's pretty. It's just strange to be out of the city."

"Manchester is a dive," Jenny said. "I swear, it's one step up from Lowell."

Brian didn't say anything.

"Come on, it's not like we moved out of Boston," she said after a minute.

"I know," Brian sighed. "I know. Anyway, what's on the agenda for tomorrow?"

"Tomorrow," she said, pulling her phone out of her jacket pocket, "let's see. Well, we have the plumber coming over at ten to give us an estimate on reworking the upstairs bath, and then we have a technician from J. Lawrence Hall coming in to make sure everything's good with the furnace."

"Is that it?" Brian asked.

"For house stuff, yeah," she answered.

"Good."

"What about work?"

"Not much," Brian answered. "I'm going to make sure the booster works for the Wi-Fi. All of the clients know they can reach me on the cell if necessary, and I'll get over to a secure facility to check on their issues."

"No physical checks this week?"

Brian shook his head. "Next week those will start back up."

"Good."

They stood for a few more minutes on the porch, watching the sun finish its descent behind the western horizon, and then Brian stretched. "Ready to go inside?"

"Yeah."

Jenny led the way back into the house, Brian closing and locking the door behind them. He shrugged off his coat and hung it up in the hall closet that smelled decidedly like too many mothballs. Jenny did the same, except her nose didn't wrinkle at the smell the way his did.

Brian glanced around at the moving boxes stacked everywhere and tried not to think about the unpacking that lay ahead of them. He started to walk towards the kitchen and then stopped.

"Babe," he said.

"Yeah?" Jenny asked, looking over her shoulder as she was closing the closet door.

"Did you go in the basement?"

"No," she said. "Why?"

"The basement door's open."

The heavy door, which Brian had closed earlier in the day, was open. Only an inch or two, but it was open.

He walked over, suddenly feeling uncomfortable. The house was warm enough, but by the door to the basement, it was cold, exceptionally cold, as if someone had left open the door to a walk-in freezer.

Even the handle was cold to the touch.

Brian closed the door and then gave the handle a gentle tug.

It didn't even rattle in the frame.

He pulled harder, and still there was only a little movement.

Beneath the old cut-glass handle was a keyhole, and Brian wondered if they had the key for that particular lock.

"Do you think it opened on its own?" Jenny asked, walking over to stand beside him.

"Maybe," Brian said. "Do you have that ring of keys that was left with the house?"

"It's in the kitchen. I'll go grab it."

Jenny left, and a minute later she called out, "Brian, did you move them off of the table?"

"I never even touched them," he called back.

After a minute, she came back, shaking her head. "I must have put them someplace else."

"Okay," Brian said, looking at the door again. "At least we have the house keys."

"Exactly. Do you want to get a fire going, and I'll get us some wine?"

Brian looked at Jenny and smiled. "Damn right, I do."

Jenny laughed and left the room to get the wine while Brian walked into the parlor, wondering where the keys might be.

## Chapter 2: Danny Sullivan's Hunting Trip

Danny was in the woods well after sunset. If a Fish and Game Conservation Officer caught him, he knew he would be royally screwed. But, from what he had heard at the Nashua Fish and Game Club, the officers had swept through Mont Vernon last week. Sure, they could change up their rhythm, but there had been a rumor of poaching in Greenfield. Danny was sure the officers would be working that area over the week.

He stepped along the path, using night-vision goggles to follow the slim game trail. Another hundred yards or so, and he'd find his trail camera and figure out if anything was coming around the salt lick he'd put out the week before. Danny paused, shifted his deer rifle from his left shoulder to his right, and debated whether or not to stop and take a leak.

*Definitely shouldn't have had those beers at Henry's,* Danny thought.

Deciding he'd go later, and not anywhere the deer might catch wind of it, Danny continued on.

A few minutes passed, and he came to the small clearing where he had set up his salt lick. His trail camera was still attached to the young elm tree he'd chosen, and Danny grinned. He opened the camera, pulled the SD card, and then dug his small digital camera out of the front pocket of his hunting jacket. Even with his gloves on, Danny managed to slide the SD card into the camera. A moment later, he flipped his goggles up and was accessing images from the trail.

Most of the initial stills were just of a raccoon passing by, but then he caught one of a good sized doe. After that, he had a pair of does, and finally a buck with a six-point rack. He checked the time-stamps on the pictures and noticed they had all been taken between six and seven PM.

*It's only quarter to six now,* Danny thought with a grin. He scanned through a couple more pictures of the wandering raccoon, one of a border collie, and then he stopped, his breath catching in his throat.

The picture showed a man. An old man with a large mustache and a broad-brimmed hat. He wore an old three-quarter length jacket and a pair of jeans with old boots, and he was staring at the deer lick.

But Danny could see through him.

The outline of the man was barely visible, and through the man, Danny could see the other side of the clearing and the distant dark shape of the old Kenyon house on the crest of a slight hill.

*What the hell?* Danny thought, finally exhaling. He flipped through the next few pictures, but saw nothing else. Shaking his head, he turned his camera off, put his goggles back down, and returned the SD card to the trail camera.

It was then he noticed there were lights on in the Kenyon house, which was another thousand yards across open ground. Danny remembered there had been talk down at Henry's that somebody had bought the place.

Turned out it was true.

*More luck to them*, Danny thought.

With a grunt, Danny walked around the edge of the glade, staying in the tree line until it cut away sharply to the right. His hide was there, and he settled down in it, getting his rifle set and making sure the safety was off. For a moment, he wondered if the new owners of the Kenyon house would be upset about him hunting on their property, and then he chuckled. He'd have a kill field dressed and ready to go long before anyone could get out to him.

Getting comfortable, he waited, neither moving nor making any sort of sound. The slight pressure of beer on his bladder vanished as he focused on the salt lick.

Minutes slid by, and Danny got in the hunting zone, perfectly happy to be doing nothing. He breathed easily, in through his nose and out through his mouth. He waited, watching.

Soon he heard a soft crunch, the faintest of sounds. Silence followed, and then a few minutes later, the deer appeared. It was a doe, and while Danny would have liked the six pointer that had shown up before, he was happy with the animal in front of him.

Lifting his goggles, Danny took a deep breath and slowly lowered his face to the stock of his rifle, the wood cold against his cheek. He looked through the night scope on the rifle. The built in light suppressor in the optics would ensure that the light of the shot wouldn't blind him. Danny watched the doe amble cautiously up to the salt and start licking it.

Smiling, he took careful aim at the shoulder of the animal, at the heart, and slowly squeezed the trigger.

The recoil on the rifle was slight, the sound brutal in the stillness of the night. The doe leaped away in fright, managed a single long step, and fell to her side.

The shot was clean.

The doe was dead.

Danny dropped his goggles into place, picked up the hot brass shell casing from the ground, slipped it into an outer pocket, and quickly collapsed the hide. He stuffed it into his shoulder bag and hurried back to the trail camera, undoing the Velcro strap and sliding the entire assembly into a side pocket on his pants. Shouldering his rifle, Danny jogged out to the doe. He dropped down to his knees, slipped his gutting knife out of its sheath on his belt, and got to work.

A few minutes into it, Danny had the doe open and the offal tossed to one side, the smell of blood hot and stinking of iron in his nose.

"Iron," a voice whispered.

Danny stiffened and looked around.

He couldn't see anything.

Suddenly uncomfortable, Danny turned back to the doe and started working on the rest of the --

"Salt," the same voice whispered.

Danny got up to his feet, took a couple of steps and looking around, he turned sharply and slipped in the doe's innards.

"Hell's bells!" Danny swore, dropping the knife so he wouldn't stab himself. He hit his head and knocked the goggles off into the doe's stomach.

"You've got to be kidding me," he groaned, already feeling the blood seeping into his pants.

"Iron and salt," the voice whispered.

Danny scrambled to his feet, slipping again in the bloody grass before he was able to stand. Twisting around, he found the speaker.

It was the old man from the picture on the trail camera, but he was still just as see through.

Danny felt a chill sweep over him as the old man looked at him with a pair of tired, hazel eyes.

"Iron and salt," the old man said once more. "Iron and salt."

Something unbearably cold wrapped around Danny's heart, squeezing it mercilessly. Danny collapsed to the ground, falling onto his left side. Unable to move, unable to breathe, he heard the old man again.

"Iron and salt."

Danny's vision slowly collapsed, the old man's face the last thing he saw.

## Chapter 3: Brian and Jenny in the House

"What the hell was that?" Jenny asked, looking up from her crochet.

Brian looked up from his book, blinked, and reran the sound through his head. "Sounded like a rifle."

"That was close by," she sighed. She looked back down at the scarf she was making.

"Yeah," Brian said. "Probably somebody poaching on our land. At least it's not some dumbass doing a drive-by with some cheap SKS on South Willow in Manchester."

"True," Jenny said. She looked over at him. "Are you going to check it out in the morning?"

Brian shook his head. "In about half an hour. If they did get something, I want to give them plenty of time to get it ready to move. After that, I'll go out there, make a lot of noise, bring the big LED flashlight. More than likely, they'll see me and hear me. Should cut down on any more poaching. If it doesn't, well, I'll fire off a few shots myself next time, let them know we're not playing around."

"Sounds good to me." Jenny grinned, blowing him a kiss.

Brian grinned and went back to his book, finishing off his second glass of wine and a few more chapters in the Dumas biography he was reading. Thirty minutes later, the mantle clock, which was one of the few items that had been unpacked, struck seven. Brian put his book down and stood up, stretching. He took his phone off of the side table, slid it into his back pocket, and walked to the hall closet.

The basement door was open again.

Frowning, he closed it, calling out to Jenny, "Hey, the basement door was open again. We'll have to get a new lock or something for it."

"Okay," she called back. "I'll put it on the list."

Brian went to the closet, dug his coat out, and took a flashlight from the bug-out bag on the closet floor. "Be back in a little while. See if I can find anything."

"Be safe."

"I will," he answered. Brian turned on the porch light, opened the door, and walked out into the cold night air. After he closed the front door, Brian stood on the porch for a few moments, getting adjusted to the cold.

It felt good.

He could smell the wood smoke from the fireplace, and under it, Brian could smell snow in the air. The sky was clear, the stars sharp and bright. The moon was nothing more than a sliver, but that too shone brightly. From somewhere nearby, possibly the old barn at the edge of their property, Brian heard an owl calling out.

*I might get used to this*, he thought. There was a definite lack of ambient noise but it felt good, in a strange way.

Nodding to himself, Brian put on his gloves, turned on the flashlight, and walked down the stairs and onto the front lawn. He closed his eyes and once more replayed the sound in his head, remembering where he had been sitting in the house.

*Not the front*, he thought. *Not the sides. Straight back, towards the woods.*

With the flashlight illuminating his steps, Brian walked around the side of the house, the grass crackling beneath his sneakers. He kept a steady pace, moving farther away from the house. The tree line was perhaps a thousand yards from the back door, and he suspected he might find the remains of a deer there. It would be the best place to wait. The deer wouldn't go out too far from the tree line, not since it was still hunting season.

The open fields would be too dangerous for them.

As Brian neared the treeline, he swept the flashlight from left to right and back again, looking for any indication someone had been around. Then, at the edge of the flashlight's range, he caught a glimpse of a salt lick and something on the ground. Brian frowned.

A deer had been baited and shot.

As he got closer to the salt lick, though, he realized there were two shapes on the ground, and while one was definitely a deer, the other shape was dressed in woodland camouflage.

"Oh shit," Brian said out loud. He broke into a trot, careful of his footing on the grass, knowing the treads on his sneakers were a little too smooth for good traction.

In a minute, he reached the body. The dead man was lying on his side in a mess of congealing blood offal. A rifle hung loosely off the hunter's shoulder, and a skinning knife was a few feet away from the open right hand. Carefully, Brian took hold of the hunter and turned the body towards him.

The look of fear and horror frozen on the man's face caused Brian's heart to skip a beat.

It looked as though the man had literally died of fear.

Brian stood up and took his phone out of his back pocket. He pulled off his right glove and dialed 911. After asking his emergency and location, the operator patched him through to Milford, the closest police department. Mont Vernon wasn't big enough for its own.

"And who is this?" the dispatcher asked after Brian told her the situation.

"Brian Roy," Brian said.

"Address, Mr. Roy?"

"One Eighty-Five Old Nashua Road, Mont Vernon," he answered.

When she asked his phone number, he rattled it off.

"Alright, Mr. Roy," she said. "You're sure the man is dead?"

"Absolutely."

"Okay. Leave the scene alone, and please wait at your house for the officers. Turn your porch light on, and all of the lights on the first floor if possible. We want to make sure they'll be able to see you."

"Understood," Brian said.

He ended the call and looked down at the body of the hunter.

"Seriously," Brian sighed, looking down at the dead hunter. "You had to do this shit on my first night here? Christ, even in Manchester, I never had a body in my backyard."

Shaking his head in disgust, Brian turned around and headed back towards the house, trying not to think of the new and inventive curses that were going to tumble out of his wife's mouth.

\*\*\*

# Moving In

At eleven thirty PM, the last of the police left the house.

Brian was tired, angry and ready to punch a cop.

Jenny, per usual, had managed to keep him cool and to keep his overworked heart from sending him to the ER.

All of the police officers who had shown up had been decent guys. All except for the last one, a blowhard part-timer who had spent twenty years in Billerica in Massachusetts. The guy thought he was tough and threw his impressive bulk around.

Brian had referred to him as Jabba when speaking to one of the other officers, and that was when Jenny had stepped in.

Brian was in his pajamas and his robe, a pair of slippers on his feet, and a much-needed glass of Booker's, neat, in his hand. He knew the police were going to be out in the backyard for a while, more than likely until the early morning. It was a crime scene, and everything had to be documented until they could get an autopsy done and officially rule out homicide.

Brian wanted to sleep.

Jenny had taken an Ambien and was already asleep upstairs. He had promised her he'd only have one drink, and he was already regretting the promise.

But he had made it, and he was going to keep it.

Brian sipped at the Bookers and closed his eyes.

This was definitely not how he wanted to spend the first night in the house. He had hoped there might be a romantic interlude at some point, but Mr. Poacher had put the squash on that.

Jenny was starting a new job in Merrimack in the morning, and she was already cutting it close with the Ambien. She'd never fall asleep without it, though; Brian could thank her ex-husband for that.

"Stop it," he muttered to himself.

Thinking like that would piss him off, and that wouldn't be any good for either of them. She had already had to bring him to Elliot Hospital for one heart attack. He didn't want her to have to bring him somewhere because of another one. And God forbid if he died on the next one.

He was sure she'd figure out a way to bring him back and kill him. More than once, too.

Smiling, Brian finished his drink and stood up. He started to carry the glass to the kitchen when he felt a cold breeze. Frowning, he turned toward it. The breeze vanished, but it had definitely come from the study Brian would be using as an office.

Walking into the study, Brian pushed the button on the old style light switch and looked around.

The room's two windows were closed, and there wasn't enough wind to force any sort of breeze down through the room's small fireplace. His boxes of office supplies and electronics were stacked on his desk, but that was all. The shelves were bare; curtains blocked the view of the world beyond the room, and everything was silent.

Shaking his head, Brian turned off the light and walked to the kitchen. He put the glass down by the sink, put the Booker's in the cabinet over the fridge, and turned the light out as he left the room. Walking down the hallway towards the stairs, he heard a click and looked back.

The light was on in the kitchen.

From upstairs, he could hear the gentle sound of Jenny snoring.

Turning around, Brian went back to the kitchen.

The Booker's was on the counter beside the glass, and there was perhaps a half an inch of the liquor in the tumbler.

A chill ran along Brian's spine, and the hair stood up on his arms.

"I finished my drink," he told the kitchen, "and I put that bottle away. I'm not doing either one of those things again."

Brian turned his back on the kitchen, turned out the light once more, and walked away. When he reached the stairs, he heard a second click.

The fear that gripped him was primal, but he turned and looked.

The kitchen light was on.

Slowly, taking deep breaths, Brian walked back to the kitchen again.

The glass was empty and stood alone by the sink.

The cabinet door over the fridge was open and showed the bottle of Booker's standing there amongst the other liquors.

"The light," Brian said after a minute, "is staying on."

He left the room and walked to the stairs again. When he placed his hand on the banister, he heard a click for the third time, and he knew, before he looked, that the light to the kitchen was off.

A quick glance showed he was right, and Brian hurried up the stairs to the bedroom. He kicked off his slippers, shed his robe, and got into bed as fast as he could. He rolled onto his right side and put his back up against Jenny's as he pulled the blankets up around him.

For the first time in a terribly long time, Brian felt the urge to pray.

# Moving In

## Chapter 4: Brian and the Furnace Technician

Brian was on his second cup of coffee, and extremely wary of the house, when the technician from J. Lawrence Hall called and said he'd be there in about half an hour.

Brian took a break from setting up his office and walked out into the hallway, glancing down at the kitchen. Nothing was going on there, so he went into the parlor. He had thought about telling Jenny what had happened in the kitchen before he went to bed, but part of him doubted what he had seen. He had enjoyed a couple of glasses of wine, and a Booker's, which was more than he usually did. Plus, there was the stress of the move and the whole dead poacher thing.

There were a lot of mitigating factors, but Brian couldn't shake the feeling something real had occurred. Why it had occurred, he had no idea. He couldn't ignore it, though.

Deciding he would bring it up to Jenny after dinner, Brian worked on his office until there was a knock at the door.

Brian called out, "Here I come." He put down his printer, wondering where the hell he'd put the damned thing's power cord.

Grumbling and shaking his head, Brian walked to the front door and opened it. A young man stood on the porch, holding a canvas tool bag in one hand and adjusting his glasses with the other.

"Brian?" the young man asked.

"Brian indeed," Brian said, extending his hand.

The young man shook it. "I'm Jack from J. Lawrence Hall. You have a furnace that needs a little attention?"

"I hope it's just a little attention," Brian said. "Come on in. The basement's this way." Brian led Jack to the basement door, which was surprisingly still closed. He opened it and turned the light on before leading the way down the narrow wooden stairs. The smell of earth and age rose up to greet him as a chill settled in around him.

"Dirt floors?" Jack asked.

"On the other side of the furnace," Brian said. "Someone put some concrete down at one point or another. Some of the piping for the furnace does run through the dirt section, though."

The basement was empty except for a few broken chairs and a half a dozen wooden apple crates that had come with the house. At the far end of the basement, under the kitchen, the furnace stood off slightly, to the left. A slim doorway was beyond the furnace, a pair of pipes branching off into the darkness.

"I don't know if there's a light in there or not," Brian said, nodding towards the doorway. "I glanced in with a flashlight when we bought the place, but that was it."

"Not a problem," Jack said. He looked around and smiled. "It's nice to work in an open area. Some people have years of stuff piled around, and others have a mess."

"I can't even imagine," Brian said.

Jack chuckled. "Good times, I'm tellin' ya."

Brian laughed and shook his head. "Okay. Listen, if you need anything, I'll be upstairs."

"Sounds good to me," Jack said, putting his bag down beside the furnace.

Brian left the young man to his work and went back to getting the office ready. The indicator on his cell was flashing when he walked into the office, and he picked the phone up off of the desk.

*Did the furnace tech show up yet?* Jenny had texted.

*He's here now. Give you an update soon,* Brian texted back.

He put the phone down, picked up his coffee, and frowned when he took a sip and realized it was cold. He carried the mug into the kitchen and put another pot of coffee on. From under the kitchen, he heard Jack working. Occasionally the pipes rattled as the young man checked something.

Soon Brian was back in the office. He found some Motorhead in his music library and dropped the phone into the docking station. In a moment, the office was filled with music, and Brian nodded along happily in time to the beat. He took a sip of his coffee and then started hunting again for the cord to the printer.

Three and a half boxes later, he found it, mixed in with a package of padded yellow mailers.

Brian held the cord up, shaking his head. "How the hell does that happen?"

"Brian!" Jack yelled from the basement.

Brian dropped the cord onto his desk, turned the music off, and hurried out of the room. Standing at the top of the basement stairs, he called down, "You okay?"

"Yeah," Jack said, appearing at the bottom of the stairs. "You may want to come and take a look at this, though."

Frowning, Brian started down the stairs.

Moving In

## Chapter 5: Officer Sal Merkins

Sal Merkins didn't believe for a minute that the new owner of the old Kenyon place had nothing to do with Danny Sullivan's death. Sal had known Danny for ten years and nothing, absolutely nothing, scared that man. There was no reason why Danny should have looked like that unless maybe somebody poisoned him.

While Sal had never gotten his detective's shield in Billerica; too much internal politics and all that crap, he'd seen some messed up murders in his twenty years. Plus, having been on his pension for the past few years, he had a hell of a lot of time on his hands. He watched a lot of television now, especially those investigative shows and the old reruns of American Justice and the FBI Files.

Sal was positive that when the autopsy was done on Danny, they'd find poison.

He knew it.

Sal was almost a hundred percent positive the new guy, Brian Roy, must have used some sort of blow gun or needle gun on Danny. Something that wouldn't be seen with a quick once over.

Sure, Danny liked to poach, but that wasn't any reason to kill the guy.

Sal sighed, shifted his vanilla frosted donut from his left hand to his right, and settled into the seat of his car. He was parked a ways off from the house, but he had seen the J. Lawrence Hall van pull in, and he was waiting for the damned thing to leave.

Sal took a bite of the donut and smiled. He knew he shouldn't eat it, with his diabetes and all, but he had been the stereotypical cop at the donut shop, and it was a hell of a habit to break.

Picking up his mug, Sal washed the bite down with a swallow of coffee, thick with Bailey's and a couple of Sweet'n Lows.

One day a week, or maybe two, off the bullshit diet his doctor put him on wouldn't kill him.

Sal finished the donut, took another drink, and put the mug down in the cup holder. He covered his mouth, belched, and glanced out into the woods to the right.

"Sweet Jesus!" he said, his heart pounding.

Thirty yards into the woods stood a boy, perhaps ten or eleven.

The boy was looking at Sal, a soft smile playing across his narrow face. The boy wore a baggy sweater and a pair of corduroy pants. His hands were in his pockets, and he had a newspaper boy hat tilted back on his head. The smile turned into a grin, and the boy took a hand out of his pocket, waving.

Sal gave a little wave back, shook his head, and turned his attention back to the Kenyon house.

*What the hell is a kid doing out on a school day?* Sal shook his head. *Must be home-schooled or whatever. Crazy people keeping their kids home.*

After a few minutes, Sal looked out the side window again.

The boy was perhaps five yards closer. When he saw Sal looking at him, the boy waved again.

Once more Sal returned the wave, feeling uncomfortable for some reason. He cleared his throat nervously, took a drink of coffee, and tried to focus solely on the house.

Only a minute or so later, though, Sal looked out the window again.

The boy was closer. Just another five yards or so, but still, he was closer.

Sal straightened up in his chair. The boy was exceptionally pale, like a prisoner who'd been hidden away for years.

Sal wondered if there was something wrong with the kid. What if he was autistic? What if he had wandered away from his house?

"Shit," Sal grumbled. He opened his door and got out, holding the door and frame to steady himself, his knee complaining, his feet tingling. Turning around to look over the roof of the car, Sal saw the boy was gone.

Sal looked to the left and to the right, but he didn't see anything.

The boy had disappeared.

"What the hell?" Sal said. He turned around and nearly fell, for the boy stood a few feet away from the car.

After catching his breath and hoping that his racing heart would calm down, Sal said, "Kid, are you okay?"

The boy smiled at Sal, nodding.

"Ah, well," Sal said, sitting back down on his seat. "That's good to hear."

The boy continued to smile, the look on his face raising the goose bumps on Sal's arms.

"So," Sal said, clearing his throat after a quick glance at the house to make sure the van was still there, "do your parents home school you?"

The boy only smiled.

"Do you go to school?" Sal asked.

The boy nodded.

"The elementary in Milford? They bus you in?"

"No," the boy said, his smile never leaving his face.

"Then where do you go to school?" Sal asked.

"My grandfather teaches me."

*Home schooled*, Sal thought. "What are you studying today?"

"History," the boy grinned. "History and the right to control."

"Oh," Sal said, "um, that's interesting."

The boy nodded.

"Where's your grandfather?" Sal asked, wondering if the man was out looking for his odd grandson.

"There," the boy pointed.

Sal looked out of the passenger side window and saw an old man standing in the forest where the boy had been a few minutes earlier. The man was grim, his face looking as though it had been beaten out of granite. His frown spoke of disappointment and sullen anger.

The man slowly faded from Sal's vision as though a soft cloud had passed over Sal's eyes. Then there was a black veil that moved across the world, blocking everything from view.

Sal tried to speak and found he couldn't. He started to shake, to tremble. Sweat burst from his skin, and his heart pounded. His tongue swelled in his mouth, and Sal found he couldn't breathe, but he couldn't move his hands to open his mouth and push his tongue aside. He fell back into the driver's seat of his car.

Sal couldn't do anything other than shake in his seat, blind to the world.

A hand caressed his cheek, the flesh so cold, Sal would have screamed if he could.

"I love staying home," the boy whispered into Sal's ear. "I learn so much."

Sal felt his legs begin to twitch violently, smashing his knees into the underside of the steering column.

The cold hand vanished from his cheek, and Sal continued to writhe in his seat.

## Chapter 6: Brian, Jack, and the Unlit Room

"You didn't check this room out at all?" Jack asked, leading the way to the dark section of the basement.

"I glanced at it," Brian said. "Why?"

"Check this out," Jack said. He walked into the small room, stepping off to the right. He was wearing a small headlamp and turned it on, the light powerful and illuminating. "Do you see where the pipes branch off to the left?"

"Yeah," Brian said. The pipes went through an opening at the top of the rocks that were part of the foundation.

"That's a false wall," Jack said excitedly.

"What?" Brian asked.

"Yeah," Jack said. "It's totally false. I went to look at the connections, you know, to shine my light in there to make sure there wasn't any rust or anything on the joints. I figured the pipes were in a little crawlspace, but no. It's all open behind this wall."

Brian stepped a little further into the room and then moved in a little further again.

Finally, Brian stepped up to the stone wall and touched it.

The wall was cold, but it surely wasn't stone. Brian gently ran his hands over the false stones and said, "It's like they were made out of papier-mache and then painted and shellacked."

"Right," Jack said. "This is crazy."

Brian nodded. He squatted down and found a single iron ring embedded in the false wall near the floor, in the absolute center. Glancing up, he saw a large iron hook hanging from the joist above him. Jack looked up, too.

"Holy shit," Jack said softly. "Do you think the wall pulls up?"

"Let's find out," Brian said. Reaching out, he took hold of the iron ring and pulled it gently. The ring came out of the wall, trailing a chain that went taut after about a foot. When Brian stood and pulled the ring up, the wall swung out and up easily, and in a moment Brian hooked the ring to the hook.

There was enough room between the bottom of the false wall and the dirt floor for both Brian and Jack to walk hunched over into a much larger space. Once they were inside the room they stood up. The hidden room was longer than Brian had suspected, perhaps eighteen feet in length and another ten feet wide. Part of it had to run beyond the house.

*Maybe an old root cellar that was converted,* Brian thought. But for what?

Jack took a step forward, looking around, his headlamp filling the room. There was no window, just stone walls and thick wooden beams, different from the rest of the basement. The heating pipes ran into the room for a few feet before turning up and into a hole in the beams and disappearing into the wall above them.

The floor, like the first part of the room, was dirt, yet there was a difference. Set into the dirt were nine stones, all flat, each of them engraved.

Brian squatted down and looked closely at the first stone, reading the inscription.

*Mary McNerney Kenyon, Beloved Wife of Josiah A. Kenyon, b. May 3rd, 1826 d. June 25th, 1876.*

"What the hell," Brian said. He stood up, looking at the familiar pattern of name, inscription, and dates on the other stones. "This is a goddamned graveyard."

"Geez," Jack said softly. "I've heard about this before."

"What?" Brian asked, turning to look at the young man.

"Yeah." Jack nodded. "New Hampshire's got this weird law, man. You can bury your family on your own property. And back in the old days, they used to bury people in the basements."

Brian rubbed the back of his head, absently reflecting that he needed to shave it again. "You know; I think somebody could have told me there were a bunch of graves in the house *before* I bought it."

"Yeah," Jack said. "Sorry, man."

"Not your fault," Brian said. "You didn't sell me the place."

"Yeah."

After a moment, Jack said, "Hey, would you mind if I snapped some pictures? Nobody is going to believe me without proof."

Brian laughed, shaking his head. "Knock yourself out, kid. I've got to go lay into my real estate agent."

"Good luck," Jack said, taking his phone off of his belt.

Moving In

"Thanks," Brian said. He made his way to his office, drank his coffee, which had cooled at record speed, and picked up his phone. He sent a text off to Jenny. *Hey, Babe, wanted to let you know there's a graveyard in the basement.*

With the text sent, Brian gave his real estate agent a call.

## Chapter 7: Trooper Waltner on Old Nashua Road

Tim Waltner was nearly done with his shift. All he needed to do was a drive-by along Old Nashua Road in Mont Vernon. A poacher had been found dead, cause not yet determined, and so the State Police wanted to let any other poachers in the area know they were around. The guys from Fish and Game would roll through during the night as an extra warning. Some of those guys seemed to like playing in the woods at night a little too much.

Nearing number 185 Old Nashua Road, Tim spotted an older model Crown Victoria parked up and off the side near the turn-around at the end of the road. The driver's side door was open, and there was someone sitting in it. The license plate read, "Merkins."

Tim rolled his eyes.

Merkins was a pain in the ass. The guy was retired. He needed to stay retired before he got himself or, more than likely, somebody else hurt.

The guy was a train wreck. Probably one step away from diabetic shock.

Slowing his patrol car down, Tim rolled down his window as he approached Merkins. When he pulled up beside the Crown Vic; though, Tim saw instantly that Sal Merkins was not in good shape. In fact, it looked like the man had gone into diabetic shock a while ago.

Tim threw his car into park and got out quickly, hurrying to the obese ex-cop. The man's eyes were closed, and his body was cold to the touch. Tim checked for a pulse in the man's wrist and in his neck.

Nothing.

On Sal's sharply creased blue pants were candy sprinkles and remnants of frosting. There was a Dunkin Donuts bag on the seat next to him. A coffee mug was in a cup holder, and the keys were in the ignition.

Sal was undeniably dead. The stench of feces and urine assaulted Tim's nose.

He stepped back, sighed, and then went back to his car to call it in.

When he was done, Tim went down to the turnaround, swung around so he was facing back down the road, and pulled the patrol car up behind the Crown Vic.

Tim parked his car, put on his lights, and took his phone out.

He could play a game or two of solitaire before the team got out to process the scene. In five minutes he would be getting paid for overtime.

## Chapter 8: Brian and Jenny at Home

"Wow," Jenny said.

Brian and Jenny stood in the hidden room, Brian holding the flashlight and showing her the headstones.

"This is crazy." she said, shaking her head.

"I know."

"Who the hell buries their family in the basement?"

"Evidently the Kenyons did."

"But what about the smell?" Jenny asked. "I mean, don't the bodies stink as they rot? Wouldn't that smell come up through the house?"

"We'll have to Google it."

"Wow," she said again. After a moment, she added, "I want to get a pen and paper later, write down everybody's names and see what I can figure out."

"Sounds good to me. Why don't we go upstairs? The meatloaf is going to be done in about ten minutes."

She looked over at him and smiled. "Okay, Mr. Domestic."

Brian chuckled.

Together they left the room, and Brian unhooked the ring, lowering the wall back into place. The last thing he wanted to hear in the night was the sound of the wall crashing down because either the ring or the hook let go.

"Did you see the ambulance over by the turnaround?" Jenny asked.

"No," Brian said. "What were they doing, hanging out?"

"No," Jenny said, shaking her head. "There was another car and a couple of state police cruisers. They all had their lights on. You didn't see anything?"

"Nope," Brian said. "I stayed in the office most of the day, and the furnace tech let himself out."

"You need to be more observant," she said, winking at him.

Which reminded him of the kitchen.

"Speaking of observant," Brian said as he led the way back upstairs, "I didn't tell you what happened last night in the kitchen after you went to bed."

"No, you didn't," she said. "What happened?"

Brian told her, finishing the story as they both walked into the kitchen.

"Are you serious?" she asked, sitting down at their small breakfast table.

"Yup," Brian said. He opened the stove door and peered in at the meatloaf, enjoying the smell. Smiling to himself, he closed the door. "It freaked me out."

"Why didn't you wake me up?" she asked.

"Two reasons," Brian said, smiling as he sat down across from her. "The first is that I wouldn't have been able to. Your Ambien is strong, Babe."

"True. What's the second reason?"

"I didn't want to have you either scared or down in the kitchen demanding that whatever it was did it again for you."

Jenny laughed, nodding her head. "Okay. Fair enough."

"I did manage to get a hold of our real estate agent when you were on your way home," Brian said.

"Oh, yeah? What did she have to say about the other tenants of the house?"

"That she didn't know about them," Brian said. "I believe her. She's pissed about it. She said she was going to ask around locally to see if anyone knew about the graves."

"I hope she finds out something," Jenny said.

"If she doesn't, I will," Brian said.

"Do you think," Jenny said after a minute, "the basement door opening and closing has something to do with the graves down there?"

"I really, really hope not," Brian said. "I know you love ghosts and supernatural stuff, and I don't mind those things, so long as they're not in the house I live in."

"Don't worry, big man," she said, grinning. "I'll protect you."

Brian chuckled and leaned back in his chair. He opened his mouth to speak, but closed it suddenly as something cold moved past him.

The grin on Jenny's face vanished.

"Did you feel that?" she asked.

Brian nodded.

"That's crazy," she said, standing up. She walked to the window and looked outside. "It's not even windy out. Not a single one of the trees is moving out there."

"I'm not surprised."

She walked back to the table, sitting down again. "Do you think that it's one ghost?"

"I have no idea," Brian said, "but I want there to be no ghosts."

"You know," Jenny said, "I should invite Sylvia Purvis over."

"No," Brian groaned. "Not Sylvia."

"She's not with Dom anymore," Jenny said, frowning slightly.

"It doesn't matter if she's with anyone or not," Brian said. "I know she's your friend, Babe, but that woman's a pain in the ass."

"Yeah, but she means well."

"Hitler meant well too."

"Oh, cut the shit." Jenny sighed. "I want to invite her over."

"Okay," Brian said. "Okay. When?"

"I'll see what she's doing tomorrow."

Brian wanted to say something snarky about Sylvia being busy doing Tarot card readings for her cat, but the timer for the meatloaf went off and saved him.

Keeping his comments to himself, and the peace of the house intact, Brian got up and put on his oven mitts.

## Chapter 9: Sylvia Pays a Visit

"Babe," Jenny said. "She'll be here in ten minutes."

Brian nodded as the clock on the mantle struck nine. He stood up, stretched, and walked out of the parlor into the kitchen. From the liquor cabinet, he took down a bottle of Jameson's, and poured half a mug full of the whiskey.

*This might be enough to deal with Sylvia.*

He capped the whiskey and left it out on the counter in case he needed more.

Jenny frowned at him as he sat down, but she didn't say anything. She knew he didn't like Sylvia. Sylvia didn't know it, but Jenny did.

Sylvia irritated him.

To the point where he occasionally fantasized about physically lifting Sylvia out of the house to make her leave when they had the misfortune of being in the same room together.

Brian put his happy face on for Jenny, though, and he bolstered that fake happiness with a long drink from his mug.

He wouldn't be drunk when Sylvia was there, but he sure as hell wasn't going to be sober either.

Twenty-five minutes later, there was a knock on the door, and Jenny put down her crochet. She got up, gave Brian a kiss on the top of his head, and made her way to the front door.

"Jenny!" Sylvia said, her voice as pleasant as a pair of tomcats fighting.

Brian took another healthy drink and realized he might have to top off his drink sooner rather than later.

Jenny walked back into the parlor with Sylvia behind her.

Sylvia was tall and strikingly beautiful. She was also insane as far as Brian was concerned. She stank of incense, wore clothes that may or may not have been washed in the past decade, and had enough bells and charms on her body that she sounded like a wind chime store caught in a hurricane.

"Hello, Brian!" Sylvia exclaimed, looking over the top of her reading glasses at him, her red hair piled high and messy on her head.

"Hello, Sylvia," Brian said.

"I love your house," Sylvia said, walking to the loveseat and sitting down, dropping her huge blue purse onto the cushion beside her.

"Thank you," Brian said. "But the house was all Jenny, not me."

Jenny smiled at him as she sat in her chair.

"So," Sylvia said, looking at Brian intensely, "Jenny told me you experienced something supernatural here?"

*Oh my God*, Brian thought. Continuing to smile, though, he said, "Yes, the other night."

"That's amazing," Sylvia sighed. "You're so fortunate. There are few people that can be open enough to engage in contact with the ethereal world. Welcome."

Brian could only nod.

"Jenny," Sylvia said, "what is it you would like me to do?"

Jenny smiled at her friend. "We want to know what, if anything, is going on in the house."

"Well, I can tell you this house is alive with energy," Sylvia said, looking around. "It's amazing."

*What's truly amazing is I'm listening to your bullshit,* Brian thought. He still smiled, though, wondering if he could slip away and get another drink.

Sylvia took her glasses off, letting them hang on her chest by a delicate chain. She closed her eyes, spread her arms out to either side and extended all of her fingers. For a few moments, she stayed that way, a small half smile playing across her face.

Then the smile faded away, and a moment after that, her face became pinched as she tilted her head to one side. Her eyes darted back and forth under her eyelids, and Brian sat up.

Sylvia's entire posture changed, her arms dropping down, and her shoulders hunched. She winced and shook her head.

With a gasp, she opened up her eyes and looked around fearfully for a moment.

"Are you alright?" Jenny asked.

Sylvia looked at her, blinked, and then slowly nodded. "Yes."

"What happened?" Jenny asked.

"I'll tell you in a minute," Sylvia said, the exuberance gone from her voice. "Did you know you have graves in this house? That there are people buried here?"

Brian looked to Jenny, his eyes widening as she shook her head in wonder.

They had both agreed not to tell Sylvia, only to speak to her about the kitchen and the liquor. Not even the chills or the opening basement door.

"Yes," Jenny said. "We found them yesterday."

"They're here," Sylvia said. "They've never left."

"Why not?" Brian asked.

"They're bound here," she said uncomfortably. "Something keeps them here."

"What?" Jenny asked. "What keeps them here?"

Sylvia shook her head. "They wouldn't say."

"You said 'them,'" Brian said. "How many of them are there?"

"Seven," Sylvia said.

"Seven?" Brian asked. "Seven?"

"That are kept here," Sylvia said, nodding. "There are two others who are not forced to be here, but they still remain."

"What the —," Brian said softly.

"So nine," Jenny said, "nine ghosts are in this house."

"At least," Sylvia agreed.

"Wait, what?" Brian said. "At least?"

"There's the possibility of more," Sylvia said, clearing her throat slightly. "There were things, people, on the periphery of my sight, but I couldn't get much from them. Mostly fear, anger, surprise. But again, I don't know if they're connected to the—"

Sylvia stopped, her eyes widening.

"Sylvia?" Jenny said.

Sylvia remained perfectly still, her eyes focused on the door.

"Sylvia?" Jenny asked again.

Brian twisted in his seat to look at the doorway. He couldn't see anything there, but the basement door was open again.

# Moving In

*I know I closed that door*, he thought. Turning back around, he looked again at Sylvia. The right corner of her mouth twitched, and she shuddered before blinking several times and nodding her head.

She looked at Brian and then at Jenny.

"You need to get salt," Sylvia said firmly. "Salt and iron."

"What?" Brian asked.

"Salt," Sylvia said. "Drive into Milford, go to the supermarket, and buy yourself boxes of kosher sea salt."

"But why?" Jenny asked.

"You're going to need to seal the doors and windows into the house with it," Sylvia said. "The thing, the person that keeps the others here, he doesn't come in often, but when he does, it can be terrible."

"What type of iron?" Brian asked, straightening up.

"Bars," Sylvia answered. "Rods. Anything long you can swing. But it has to be iron. It can't be steel. Just iron."

"Why iron?" Brian asked.

"I can't explain right now," Sylvia said. "There's too much. But you have to get those things, do you understand me? You have to."

"Yes," Jenny said. "Yes, Sylvia, we'll get those things. But I thought ghosts can't hurt people?"

Sylvia looked at Jenny hard, and for the first time Brian, even through his slight haze of whiskey, realized there was some substance and backbone to Sylvia.

"Ghosts can kill people, Jennifer," Sylvia said softly but firmly. "They can literally scare you to death. They can cause things to happen. There are a great many deaths attributed to natural causes and to household accidents that are, quite simply, murders. Committed by the dead, but murders nonetheless. If you're going to stay here, you need to be prepared to defend yourselves and to find a way to get rid of the one who is binding the others here."

"What about an exorcism?" Brian asked.

Sylvia shook her head. "You don't have a demon here, Brian. You have a malicious, murderous ghost. You can destroy it. You can chase it away yourself, but an exorcism, regardless of the faith of the exorcist, will not work. This is not a matter of faith, not religious good versus religious evil. This is your straight up run-of-the-mill evil, the neighbor next door who decides killing is the most fun he's ever had."

"Great," Brian sighed. Taking a deep breath, with his hand shaking ever so slightly, Brian finished the last of his whiskey and whispered, "That's just great."

## Chapter 10: Samuel Hall Goes for a Walk

Samuel Hall had turned eighty in August, and all of those eighty years, save for a couple when he patrolled the DMZ in Korea, he had lived in Mont Vernon. Specifically, he had lived at 99 Old Nashua Road, and once he had turned sixty-eight and retired from the State's Department of Highway Maintenance, Samuel had started walking.

He walked every day.

At six o'clock in the morning, he stepped outside of the large farmhouse his great-grandfather had built, lit his first pipe of the day, and walked to the end of the driveway. From there Samuel turned left, walking the full two miles down to where Old Nashua Road intersected Route Thirteen. Once at Thirteen, Samuel turned around and walked back up Old Nashua Road, past his own home half a mile up to the turnaround, past the Kenyon House, and home again.

Samuel walked this route twice a day, at six o'clock in the morning and six o'clock in the evening. Florence, before she had passed away, had walked with him, and he often thought about his wife as he walked.

Yet when Samuel passed by the Kenyon house, he thought of Paul Kenyon, his best friend who had passed away when they were kids in 1945. Paul had been trying to climb the roof of the house again and had fallen, his grandfather finding the boy's body.

Now, after a five-day stay in the VA hospital in Manchester, Samuel was walking once again. His knees were feeling better after the cortisone injections the doctors had finally settled on. Samuel drew on his pipe, letting a long stream of smoke out into the night sky, and shook his head at the minor ordeal the hospital visit had been.

Yet as he neared the Kenyon house on the darkened road, he saw a pair of cars in the driveway and lights on in the house.

Samuel slowed down, looking as he went. No one had lived long in the house since seventy-five, when Mr. Kenyon, Paul's grandfather, had passed away. A few people had rented the home from a Kenyon cousin who lived down in Boston, but they never stayed. Then, after nine eleven, the word passed through town that the cousin had been on one of the planes that hit the towers. Since then, the cousin's estate had been trying to sell the house.

*Looks like they finally did*, Samuel thought. He turned his attention back to his walk, the flashlight he held in his gloved right hand lazily splashing light across the road and the trees. Hunting season made Samuel especially wary, and he hoped—although not with much confidence—that hunters from Nashua or Manchester understood that deer didn't move around with flashlights.

Nearing the turnaround, the flashlight flickered like a candle guttering out, and by the time Samuel reached the turnaround, the flashlight was dead. Samuel came to a stop, turned the flashlight on and off several times, and frowned. He had just put new batteries in the damned thing.

"You're old," a soft voice said. Laughter followed the statement.

Samuel looked up sharply, clenching the pipe's stem between his teeth. He searched for the source of the voice and saw a small shape near the woods on his left. The moon was only half-full, yet it cast enough light onto the road for Samuel to realize it was a child who stood perhaps twenty yards away.

"I am indeed old," Samuel said around the pipe. "And without a flashlight that works."

"You can't get home without a flashlight?" the child asked in a mocking tone.

Samuel realized the child was a boy and said, "No, young sir, I'm sure I can get home without a flashlight. I'm merely concerned about hunters. You should be too, out in the dark during hunting season."

"There aren't any hunters here," the boy replied. His voice was full of confidence. "I scared them all away, Sammy."

Samuel stiffened slightly.

No one had called him Sammy for decades, and the voice, Samuel realized with growing horror, was that of Paul Kenyon.

The pipe nearly fell from Samuel's mouth as he asked, "Paul?"

The child moved closer, and Samuel saw it was Paul. The boy wore his favorite sweater and had his hat on in its usual rakish back-tilt.

Yet Paul was dead. Samuel knew he was dead.

"Am I dying?" Samuel asked, looking at his childhood friend. "Have you come for me?"

Paul looked surprised, and then he grinned. "No, Sammy. I wanted to say hello. I've seen you walking many nights, but I was lonely tonight, and I wanted to say hello. You're not going to die. Well, at least not tonight."

Samuel shook his head, laughing. It was Paul. Then his thoughts sobered, and Samuel asked, "Are you stuck here? Can't you leave?"

The grin dropped from Paul's face. "No. I cannot leave."

"Why?" Samuel asked.

Paul shook his head, and then he smiled. "It's good to see you, Sammy. But you sure are old."

"I'm eighty now, Paul," Samuel said, smiling sadly. "I have children of my own. Grandchildren too. I did not like growing up without you."

"I will see you again, Sammy," Paul said.

Samuel watched as Paul started to fade, and then suddenly vanished altogether.

For a long, long time, Samuel stood at the turnaround. By the time he started back towards home, his pipe had gone out, and the cold air bit sharply as tears dried upon his cheeks.

## Chapter 11: Brian in the Parlor

The mantle clock struck twelve. Midnight. The witching hour.

Brian sat alone in the parlor, his Kindle on his lap as he pinched the bridge of his nose. He was tired, but he needed to know what the hell was going on. He needed to know why Sylvia had told them to get salt and iron.

When Jenny had gone to bed at eleven, Brian had started his research, hunting for information on the internet. Every somewhat decent website had directed him towards one book about ghosts, written by a James Patrick Moran in 1972.

Brian had found a Kindle version and downloaded it, and for the past forty minutes, he had been reading steadily. Neither salt nor iron could kill a ghost if kill was even the right word. Salt, however, especially sea salt that had been blessed by a Catholic or Orthodox Priest or an Orthodox Rabbi, could stop a ghost from entering a domicile. The way to do that was to place a continuous line across every door or window threshold. The lines had to be continuous, though. That was the key. Any sort of break, and the ghost could slip through.

The book didn't explain the mechanics of it, and Brian didn't want to try. He was still having a difficult enough time grasping that he had his own little cemetery.

Brian had looked up the purpose of iron, too.

Iron, for some reason, broke the ghost up, scattering its parts everywhere and forcing the ghost to focus on rebuilding itself. Any type of iron would do. The author of the book had written that the trench raiders of the First World War carried cudgels with iron-spiked heads not only to brain their opponents, but also to deal with the thousands of ghosts that wandered No Man's Land. The author suggested that anyone wishing to arm themselves against ghosts could follow the lead of the soldiers, or they could, go to scrap yards to search for something more suitable for their own size and ability. Finally, the book advocated carrying brass knuckles made of iron rather than brass as a weapon of last resort.

Brian wasn't exactly thrilled with any of it, and he was seriously wondering if it was necessary, or if Sylvia was jerking them around, when something flickered by the doorway into the hall.

Looking over, Brian didn't see anything, but he heard a click, and light spilled into the hall from the direction of the kitchen.

Brian's heart pounded fiercely, threatening him with another trip to the ER.

Taking deep breaths to slow down his mutinous heart, Brian put his Kindle on the couch and stood up. Walking carefully, he made his way to the kitchen, where he stopped abruptly in the doorway.

In front of him was the faint image of a small woman dressed in clothes that were probably in style during the Civil War. She had her back to him, and she was doing something at the counter near the sink. Brian could hear her humming softly to herself.

She turned around, capping a bottle of liquor, and smiling cheerfully at him. She was in her late forties, perhaps early fifties.

Brian watched her walk to the liquor cabinet and put the bottle away. Then she turned back to face him. She gestured towards the sink.

A tumbler half filled with liquor stood there.

Clearing his throat, Brian asked softly, "That's for me?"

She nodded.

"Thank you," Brian managed. He walked cautiously to the sink, picked up the tumbler, and took a small drink. He smiled and said, "My name's Brian."

"Mary," the woman said softly, and she vanished.

Brian tightened his grip on the tumbler to make sure he didn't drop it. Swallowing nervously, he took a long, long drink.

*Mary*, Brian thought. *Mary.*

That had been the name on the first headstone in the basement.

Mary.

Moving In

## Chapter 12: The Barn

"What's the plan for today?" Jenny asked. She stood at the front door, getting her shoes on and glancing over at him.

"The plan is to avoid all supernatural contact," Brian said. He was tired and upset, and a little disgruntled. Jenny didn't seem half as bothered as he was about the ghost situation.

"Nothing else?" she asked with a smile.

Brian shook his head. "I got the rest of the office set up yesterday, so I'm going to enjoy this last day off before jumping back into work. I'm thinking about taking a walk around the property, maybe look at the barn."

"Be careful in the barn," Jenny said, straightening up. "The thing looks like it'll fall down any time now."

"I'll be careful."

She walked over to him and gave him a kiss. "Don't worry about the ghosts, Babe. I'm sure Sylvia was blowing stuff out of proportion again. Love that girl, but she needs to tone it down sometimes."

Brian nodded. For a moment, he thought of telling her about Mary, but he decided against it. Jenny didn't need the distraction at work.

"Are you okay?" she asked.

"Yeah," Brian said. "I didn't sleep well."

"The cold air will wake you up," she said, smiling. "Have a good day. I love you."

"Love you too, Babe," Brian said. He held the door for her as she left, waving to her once she got into her car. He closed the door as she backed out of the driveway.

After putting on his coat, hat, and gloves, Brian walked onto the porch. Frost shone in the early morning sun, slowly melting, steam rising up from individual blades of grass. He looked around, deciding on whether to walk the property first or to take a look inside the barn.

The barn, a faded red and leaning slightly to the right, held far more interest to him than a mere walk.

On the way, the grass crunched loudly beneath his feet. The partially opened barn doors loomed larger as he approached.

Soon Brian came to a stop before the doors and peered inside. The sun streamed in through holes in the roof and gaps in the wooden siding. He could see stalls for horses and cattle, and in the cold air, he could smell, ever so faintly, old hay.

Smiling, Brian stepped into the barn, casting a wary eye up at the beams. Satisfied that he wasn't going to die from falling debris, he made his way deeper into the barn. Here and there, cracked and battered leather tack hung on nails driven into the beams. At the far end of the barn stood a second set of doors, these were also slightly open. Yet the small door on the far left was closed.

Brian walked to the door and saw there was a set of 'L' brackets on the door frame. Beside the door was a long, thick wooden beam.

Something had been locked in the room.

A simple wooden handle was attached to the door's exterior, and Brian took hold of it and pulled.

The door opened easily, revealing a room lit by a window high above the ground. The room was small and had a bunk across the far wall. Beneath the bunk were old toys—cars and trucks made of wood, metal soldiers Brian was sure were made of lead. The walls were covered with drawings of horses. On the bunk itself was a length of old, heavy chain, each end equipped with a manacle. An iron ring was sunk into one of the beams near the bunk, and Brian realized, with a sickening turn of his stomach, that a child was kept in the room.

Chained to the wall.

Brian stepped further into the room and picked up the chain.

It was heavy.

No child would have been able to move far around the room in the chains, even if the child wasn't shackled to the wall.

Something struck the side of the barn.

It sounded like a rock.

Brian frowned, listening.

A moment later the sound came again, a little louder.

*What the hell?* Brian thought.

Still holding the chain, he walked out of the small room and into the main part of the barn again. He listened.

Nearly a minute had passed before the sound occurred once more.

Something had struck the barn on the left side, near the front doors.

Brian gripped the chain tightly. He was going to have to let people know he owned the house now, and they needed to stop screwing around on his property. It was bad enough the hunter had died. He didn't need anything else to happen.

Walking towards the front of the barn, Brian heard a sound behind him, and he stopped.

Someone had coughed.

Brian turned around, lifting the chain up, and stopped.

An old man stood in front of him.

An old dead man, since Brian could see the back set of doors through him.

"Go back to the house," the old man said, his voice faint. "Go back to the house."

"Why?" Brian asked, lowering the chain.

"You've got the iron," the old man said. "Go get the salt."

Brian looked at the chain and realized the old man was right. The chain was iron. To the old man, Brian said, "I don't have any salt yet."

"You need to go get it," the man said. "You need to get it now."

"Okay," Brian said, not feeling good about the urgency in the man's voice. "Okay. I'll get it now."

There was the sound of another rock against the side of the barn followed by the sound of the barn doors sliding open completely, the old wheels screaming in their tracks.

"Too late," the old man said sadly.

Brian turned around quickly and saw a shape in the open area.

"Good morning, Grandfather," the shape said, stepping forward, revealing itself to be a little boy. The child smiled cheerfully at Brian and the old man behind him.

"Were you trying to save someone else, Grandfather?"

The ghost behind Brian didn't answer, and Brian didn't risk a look back. Tightening his grip on the chain, his hands sweating in his gloves, Brian looked at the boy.

"How very noble of you, Grandfather," the boy said, grinning at Brian and taking a small step forward. "How very, very noble of you."

## Chapter 13: Getting out of the Barn

The boy grinned, and Brian was sure that the grin did not translate into anything pleasant for him.

There was something wrong with the boy, above and beyond the fact that he was obviously dead.

"You're the new man living in the house," the boy said, looking at Brian. "Do you like the house?"

"Yes," Brian said, carefully.

"So do I," the boy said, cheerfully.

Brian watched him take a few steps closer.

"I like the house so very much. Do you know I died right outside the house?" the boy asked.

Brian shook his head.

"It's true," the boy said with feigned solemnity. "Right out there on the back lawn. I fell from the roof. Do you know why I fell?"

"No," Brian said.

"Good, because it's a secret; my secret," the boy snickered. "Maybe I'll tell you soon. Maybe I'll even show you."

From behind him, Brian heard the old man say, "Get to the house."

Instead, Brian took a deep breath and stepped toward the boy.

The boy's grin widened, his form taking on more definition. "Yes. Come closer."

Brian took another step forward, and the boy, still grinning, reached out for him.

Fear beat at Brian as he hefted the chain up and round over his shoulder and sent the rest swinging toward the boy. The heavy iron chain crashed down on the floor and dust erupted into the air. It had passed right through the boy without touching him.

Yet the child screamed, a cry of pure rage and hatred, and then vanished as quickly as he had appeared. Brian sagged with relief and closed his eyes, thankfully. But he wasn't given the time to collect his thoughts.

"Run!" the old man yelled, causing Brian to start again. "He'll be back soon, and angry. Get to the house and find the salt!"

Bundling the chain up in his arms, Brian ran, his vision blurred, his heart racing.

He had seen evil on that boy's face. The boy wanted to hurt him. The boy wanted to torment him before he died.

Brian considered that being dead on the ground from a heart attack was better than being dead at the hands of the evil little thing in the barn.

Brian raced up the front stairs, onto the porch and slammed his shoulder into the door as he pushed his way in. He kicked the door shut behind him, and hurried into the kitchen and looked around for salt. Any type of salt. A frantic search turned up nothing and Brian turned his attention to the pantry.

Opening the narrow door, he found a full box of sea salt.

*Why the hell didn't I dig this shit out when Sylvia said to?* Brian asked himself.

*Because you still thought that she was full of it.*

Brian didn't bother to check if it was kosher, carrying it and the chain into the parlor. Once in the parlor, Brian took a deep breath and tried to remember what Sylvia had said.

*The doorways and the windows.*

Brian put the chain on the floor, it had become heavier the longer he carried it around. He opened the salt and got down on his knees, hands shaking as he poured a line of salt from one edge of the door frame to the other. Swallowing nervously, he stood up and worked his way round all the windows in the house, making sure each was locked before carefully pouring salt along the sills.

Brian brought the box to his chair, put it down on the floor beside it, and then went and retrieved the iron chain.

Holding cold metal in his hands, Brian sat down in his chair. Exhaustion washed over him, and he realised he was sweating. How was he going to explain to Jenny what had happened in the barn?

## Chapter 14: Samuel Hall Does Some Thinking

Samuel Hall sat on his back porch and looked out at the apple orchard that ran along the edge of his property. It was always pretty to look at that time of the morning.

Most of Sam's acreage was bordered by the Greeley's Farm, the migrant workers having picked the trees clean throughout the season. Now the men had returned to wherever they had come from before the cold New England winter hit.

A smile twitched on Sam's face. He didn't mind winters too much. Maybe a little more now that he was older, but he didn't have thin blood. He wasn't like some of the men who'd come back from fighting the Japanese in the Pacific.

His older brother Thomas had been like that. Couldn't stand the cold after the war, feet rotting with some foreign fungus and a godforsaken parasite in his gut.

It was no wonder the man had drunk himself to death.

*Pretty glum today, aren't we?* Sam said, to himself.

He nodded, relit his pipe and watched the apple trees as they moved stiffly in the cold breeze.

His mind was awash with old memories he no longer knew he had. Running into the ghost of his best friend, the one who'd died all those years ago, wasn't an everyday occurrence.

Sam sighed, let out a long stream of bluish pipe smoke into the air and tapped his fingers on the arms of the chair.

Was he going mad, he wondered? It was possible. His father had. Thomas hadn't been particularly sane either, but then again, Thomas's problems had been blamed on the war. Sam even had an uncle, Joseph, who he could only remember meeting twice who'd eventually ended up in the State Mental Hospital in Concord, New Hampshire.

The chance that he might be mad rather than having actually had a conversation with Paul wasn't exactly a cheerful thought. But it was better than the notion that Paul was now a ghost.

*Why can't Paul leave?* Sam thought. *He said he couldn't leave. Why not? Who's keeping him here? What's keeping him here? Is he trapped?*

He smoked his pipe for a few minutes, more, rolling the idea around, wondering who it might be. Both of Paul's parents had died in an explosion, something wrong with the new Ford Paul's father had purchased after the war ended. Could Paul's parents be keeping him from moving on? Were they unable to move on, and were they the ones keeping Paul trapped?

Could it be Paul's grandfather?

The old man had outlived the entire family. Sam remembered him, a tired man living out each day in solitude on the farm.

*I need to find out,* Sam thought. *I have to find out how to release Paul. Set him free and get him on his way to where he should be.*

Sam nodded to himself.

*Yes. I need to do that.*

There were new people in the Kenyon house now. Perhaps they would let him look around, look for some sort of clue. If they did, maybe Sam could find something and bring the information to someone who knew what they were doing.

Someone who would know how to set Paul free.

Sam relaxed back in his chair, and refilled his pipe.

*Well,* Sam thought, tapping the tobacco down into the bowl, *maybe I'll go over to the Kenyon's first thing after lunch.*

## Chapter 15: Meeting the Neighbor

After an hour, Brian had managed to calm down enough to leave the parlor. He brought the chain with him to his office, put it down on the floor by his desk and rummaged deliberately through a box of knick knacks he hadn't put out yet.

He found what he was looking for, a cast iron piece of 'grapeshot' from the Civil War. One of his customers in Georgia had given him a collection of six pieces for having developed a security system to protect the man's disturbingly large collection of Civil War memorabilia. Brian wasn't particularly fond of the piece of grapeshot, but it sure as hell fit nicely into the palm of his hand.

Brian had a good feeling that if he held the grapeshot and punched the dead little shit, well, then the grapeshot would work just as well as the chain.

At least, he was hoping it would work just as well.

Brian was holding onto the grapeshot and checking his email when the doorbell rang.

Frowning Brian stood up and went to the door, asking, "Who is it?"

"My name is Sam Hall, I'm your neighbor from up the way. I was stopping by to ask a favor of you."

*Christ, I hope he's not dead*, Brian thought. "Sure, Sam, hold on."

Brian unlocked the door and pulled it open.

An old man stood on the porch, neatly dressed and well groomed.

"Sam Hall," the man said, extending his hand.

"Brian Roy," Brian replied, shaking the offered hand.

Sam opened his mouth to say something, but then he closed it, his eyes widening.

Brian turned slightly and saw the basement door swinging open and coming to a stop. Brian sighed as he looked back at Sam.

"Don't mind the door," Brian said, motioning for Sam to come in. "Someone thinks that it's funny to keep opening the door."

"There's no one there," Sam said as Brian closed the front door and locked it.

"No," Brian agreed. "No one I can see. Can you see anyone?"

Sam shook his head.

Brian shrugged. "Oh well. At least, it's not just me. Come on into the parlor, Sam. Just mind the salt."

"Why is there salt on the floor?" Sam asked as they entered the parlor and Brian sat down in his chair.

"Have a seat," Brian said. As Sam sat down on the sofa, Brian said, "There's salt on the floor because ghosts can't cross it."

"Oh," Sam said, looking around the room. "And that's why there's salt on the windowsills?"

Brian nodded. He didn't care if Sam thought he was crazy. Brian had thought Sylvia was crazier than a loon, until the night before.

"So, Sam," Brian said, shifting the piece of grapeshot from his left hand to his right. "What is it I can do for you?"

"Well," Sam said, "I was going to ask if I could have a look around the place. I was going to tell a bit of a lie and say it was because I haven't been in here since I was a boy, but that would only have been a partial truth."

"What's the whole truth?" Brian asked.

"The whole truth is I saw the ghost of my best friend last night when I walked by the house. I didn't think you'd let me look if I mentioned ghosts." Sam looked over at the salt and shook his head. "I suppose it's not an issue, though."

"It's not. Did you grow up around here?"

"Right down the road," Sam answered. "Born there, raised there. Family's been in that house for a long, long time. My best friend lived here. Boy, my own age named Paul."

Brian felt an uncomfortable chill run along his spine. "And you haven't been back in the house since you were a boy?"

Sam shook his head. "The last time I stepped foot in here was for Paul's wake," Sam said looking about the room. "They had the casket in here, by the fireplace. He had fallen off of the roof. God only knows what he was doing up there, but Paul was always wild."

"So Paul died when he was young?"

"Yes."

"I don't suppose he liked to wear a big sweater, and a hat tilted back on his head?" Brian asked softly.

"Yes," Sam said excitedly. "Yes, he did. In fact, he was wearing those things last night when I saw him. You've seen him then?"

"I did."

"When?"

"This morning."

"Where?" Sam asked, leaning forward. "Where did you see him?"

"Out in the barn," Brian answered. "Out in the barn where he was going to kill me."

## Chapter 16: Sam Gets a Shock

"What?" Sam asked, looking at the pale young man sitting across from him.

"He was going to kill me," Brian answered. "I bumped into him and his grandfather when I was out there looking around this morning."

"His grandfather?" Sam asked. "A tall man kind of stern looking?"

"Him to a tee."

Sam frowned. "That man loved Paul. He loved him as if he were his own son."

"They didn't seem particularly fond of one another out there in the barn this morning," Brian said. "Your friend Paul seemed fairly upset. He didn't want his grandfather saving me."

*Why would the old man be here still?* Sam wondered. *Is he keeping Paul here?*

"Are you sure he wanted to kill you?" Sam enquired. An uneasy thought crossed his mind.

"Sure as hell seemed like he had death on his mind," Brian answered. "I was lucky, though. A friend of my wife's came by. She told us about iron and salt. Iron hurts them, and the salt stops them coming into the house. I found some iron chains in the barn. Manacled chains. If it wasn't for them, you'd be talking to my ghost right now."

Sam had spent hundreds of hours as a boy in it, and there had never been any iron chains. Tack, yes. Brass for the horses, yes. But no iron chains. Maybe some steel, but not iron.

"Wait here a moment," Brian said, standing up. The young man looked nervously out into the hall, and then he chuckled. "You know, my wife's friend said that the bad one doesn't come into the house often, but when he does it's not good. Let's hope he doesn't come in now."

Brian left the room, and Sam was alone in the parlor.

Sam looked at the fireplace. He could remember distinctly the table covered in black crepe paper. Paul's coffin had looked huge and foreboding, of course. Sam remembered it all through his child self's eyes.

Moving In

The coffin had been small, and it had seemed strange that Paul had managed to fit into it. He had always seemed so much taller, somehow. What a terrible day it had been.

Paul's grandfather had stood stoically by the corner hutch in a black suit, the uniform of a hundred previous funerals, not one he should have had to bury his own grandson in. Sam couldn't remember the grandfather speaking a single word. A few of Paul's maternal aunts had organized the wake, made sure people knew, stocked the kitchen and pantry. Paul's grandfather had doted on the boy, perhaps one of the reasons why Paul was so wild at times.

"Here they are," Brian said, walking back into the room and interrupting Sam's thoughts.

Sam looked over, and he shivered at the sight of the chains in Brian's hands.

Sam suddenly remembered the chains. They weren't farm chains. They were slave chains. Paul's father had found them in Portsmouth in an old warehouse.

Sam could remember them hanging in the barn with a sign, "Remember the Yoke of Slavery." Paul's father had always been a man who favored equality.

"You found those in the barn?" Sam asked as Brian sat down.

"I did."

"Hanging up under a sign that said 'Remember the yoke of slavery?'"

Brian shook his head.

"Whereabouts did you find them?" Sam asked, frowning.

"In the small room with the lock on it."

"Ah, the tack room," Sam said, nodding, remembering the layout of the barn.

"Not unless tack means prison cell."

"What?"

"That room," Brian said, "was a place where someone was kept locked up. From the size of the room and the toys in it, I'm sorry to say it was probably your friend."

"Do you mind if I look?" Sam asked after a moment.

"Knock yourself out," Brian said, putting the chains down by his feet. "You'll forgive me if I don't join you. I don't think your friend's particularly fond of me."

"I don't know what to think," Sam said, standing up. "I saw him yesterday evening on the border of the property down at the turnaround. He was my friend. The boy I remembered."

"You may be important to him," Brian reasoned, "but I'm definitely not. Anyway, if you want to talk some more, or have a drink, come on back. I'll be making my way to the kitchen once I get a little more courage up."

"I will," Sam said, nodding. He left the parlor and the house and in a moment, he was walking to the barn, and soon he stood inside of it. He could smell old hay and horses, the smells of his childhood and youth. At the far end of the barn stood the tack room.

Sam walked to the open door and looked in.

The room was exactly how Brian had described it. Toys, wooden cars, and trucks Paul's grandfather had carved.

Drawings of horses covered the walls, and there too Sam saw the grandfather's hand. The man had been able to draw, to paint. Paul's grandfather had been able to create pictures of amazing accuracy and depth, realistic and powerful.

Sam saw the bunk at the far end, the high window above it would have allowed light to pour in. The bunk was wide and would have been able to hold the old down mattress Sam had slept on when he stayed the night at the Kenyon house. Sometimes Sam had wanted to bring the mattress home since it had been more comfortable than his own.

Paul's grandfather had changed the tack room into a cell, but he had made it as comfortable as he could.

"Nice, isn't it, Sam?" a voice asked behind him.

Sam's heart missed a beat, and he turned around. Paul sat on the dirt floor behind him, smiling.

"Grandfather tried very hard to make me comfortable."

"Why?" Sam managed after a minute.

"Why?" Paul smiled happily. "Because certain things, Sammy, certain things are fun to do."

Paul got to his feet, his smile wide in a way that frightened Sam. Only a few times in their childhood had Paul gotten mad, it was rare, blessedly rare. Because when he was angry, Paul had smiled in that same way.

"I like to do certain things," Paul said softly. "I love to do them. I feel when I do them. Even now, even dead. It's so much fun, Sammy."

Sam watched Paul's hands open and close repeatedly, and Paul's chest rose and fell rapidly.

"You need to leave, Sam," Paul said after a moment, clenching his small hands into fists. "You need to leave now. Don't come back to the farm. You stay on your side of the street. You're not a boy anymore. I don't like grown-ups."

Paul took a step closer, his translucent body seeming to glow.

"I don't like grown-ups."

Sam turned around and left the barn. If he had still been young enough to run he would have.

## Chapter 17: Brian is Alone Again, Almost

After half an hour Brian figured out Sam had gone home without calling back to the house to say goodbye. The alternative wasn't something he wanted to focus on. Part of him knew he should check the barn to make sure Sam wasn't out there, either dead or hurt, but he couldn't.

He was too afraid of the killer ghost lurking around the property.

Brian knew he couldn't hide in his parlor for the rest of the day, no matter how frightened he might be of some little sociopathic ghost. Taking a deep breath, Brian picked up the grapeshot and walked out of the parlor, carefully stepping over the line of salt in the doorway.

He paused in the hallway long enough to close the basement door and then he made his way to the kitchen. He made himself a cup of coffee, fought the urge to add a little whiskey to it and brought the drink to his office.

Once in the office, he sat at his desk, took a sip of coffee before putting the mug down and then set the piece of iron on the desk too.

Focusing on his computer, Brian tried to work.

He couldn't.

He couldn't focus on anything.

Brian drummed his fingers on the top of the desk, tapped a pen on the edge of his keyboard and thought about what he should do. The tiny bit of iron he had found was great, but was it enough?

A flicker caught his eye.

Brian paused, his fingers just barely resting on the keyboard. He looked to the doorway and saw the basement door was open. Not by much, maybe an inch or so, but it was open.

He lifted his fingers off of the keyboard and cracked his knuckles. His eyes never left the doorway, but nothing moved. The door to the basement remained open.

*Did I really see something?* Brian thought.

*Probably.*

His hands shook slightly as he went back to work.

Again something flickered, and he looked up quickly.

The hem of a dress vanished to the right.

Brian cleared his throat and asked, "Mary?"

Nothing.

Brian's scalp seemed to crawl, his skin tingling. Was it Mary? Wouldn't she have stopped and waved?

"How the hell do you know what she'll do?" he asked himself with a bitter laugh.

Shaking his head Brian tried to pay attention to his work. He opened a new email, tried to --

The computer flickered and powered down suddenly.

The light on the desk turned off, and the room was lit solely by the sun coming in through the tall windows.

The door to the office closed, the click of the lock painful to Brian's ears.

Something was in the room with him.

Something, or someone.

Brian really didn't know how to describe it even to himself.

The room grew colder, his hands starting to ache. Within a few moments, Brian could see his own breath.

"Who's here?" he managed to ask.

He received no answer.

The window on the right suddenly glazed over, ice crystals racing across the glass.

Brian turned in his chair, taking hold of the piece of grapeshot as he felt the cold intensify. The second window glazed over as well. The cold moved around him, ending in front of the desk.

He struggled to keep his heart from racing.

"Who's here?" he asked again.

Someone whispered yet Brian couldn't make out the words.

"Who?"

"Elizabeth," the voice hissed in his ear.

Brian stiffened, shaking slightly.

"Elizabeth," the voice said again.

With a shuddering breath, Brian asked, "Do you need anything, Elizabeth?"

"Pain," the voice answered.

"You're in pain?" he asked.

Something terribly cold burned into the back of his hand.

"Free me."

"How?"

"Free me."

"I don't know how," Brian said, shaking his head.

A shriek pierced his ears, and the bulb in the lamp exploded, shards of glass cutting through the shade and slashing across his face.

"God damn it!" Brian shouted, turning his head.

The door flew open, bouncing off of the wall.

The cold disappeared. Warmth returned.

"Screw this," Brian said, standing up, touching the cuts on his face gently. "I'm tired of this bullshit. I need some whiskey and some goddamned iron. This is my house now."

# Moving In

## Chapter 18: Samuel and the Deaths

Had Paul Kenyon been a murderer when he was alive? Was he still one now?

Sam sat in his armchair, smoking his pipe, and pondered the questions. The smoke curled around him, and Sam looked at the dark television screen in front of him.

Could Paul have killed people, before he had died?

Was that even possible?

Sam tried to remember everything about the boy he had known.

Yes, Paul's temper had been frightening. Yet not too frightening since it had never been directed at Sam.

Paul didn't like grown-ups. Paul never had.

Sam thought back to his childhood. It seemed so long ago.

Paul had loved it when they could get into Wilton on a Saturday morning and make it to the movie house. The two of them would spend all day in the theater, watching the cartoons and the serials, and being mesmerized by the newsreels about the war while it was being fought.

Paul had loved the combat footage.

Sam had also enjoyed it, not really seeing it for what it was, not really knowing what horrors could be found in war.

Perhaps Paul had truly loved the carnage of it all.

The idea bothered Sam.

Sam tried to remember the past for what it had been, not what he would rather it had been:

The hired hand who had scolded Paul for going into a stall with a wild horse. The man had left the farm abruptly afterward, leaving his meager belongings behind.

A maid who sickened and had to be brought down to Boston, where she had barely survived her unknown illness.

Paul's parents.

*Paul's parents.*

Sam closed his eyes, horror sweeping over him.

Yes. Paul could have easily murdered his own parents.

How the boy would have gone about the task, Sam didn't know, but he knew Paul would have found a way to do it. Paul had never liked the rules his parents had attempted to enforce. Paul had, in fact, only ever listened to his grandfather.

*But why is he here? Why hasn't Paul moved on? Has he killed others?*

Sam felt certain he had. Over the decades, people had been found dead around the farm, but always from natural causes. Hell, there had even been that poacher who died of a heart attack the other night.

Sam stood up and left the room, walking to the front hall to fetch his jacket and a cane. He felt awful, and he wanted a walk. Regardless of the threat Paul represented, Sam was going to go for his walk. He was going to smoke his pipe.

Paul Kenyon would not frighten him away from the thing Sam loved to do.

Sam would walk.

He closed the door behind him, heading out into the early evening, fighting the growing unease building within.

## Chapter 19: Brian and the Graveyard

*My mom called. She needs my help. Be home a little after seven.*

Brian had a good buzz on when the text came through a little before five. He sent a simple, *Okay,* in response and poured himself another whiskey.

His face was flushed, and he was a little dizzy even holding onto the edge of the counter. He left the whiskey open by the sink, unsure whether or not Mary would put the bottle away, although he no longer really cared whether she would or she wouldn't

*I need to know what's going on,* Brian thought. *I need to know if they're down there still. Did they leave?*

Brian finished off his drink, put the glass by the bottle and turned to look down the hallway towards the basement door.

He had closed the door before entering the kitchen and in a moment, he would see if it had remained closed.

Carefully, his balance skewed slightly from the alcohol, Brian left the room.

A nervous laugh slipped out as he caught sight of the open basement door.

The lights were on, and Brian thought he heard something as he started down the stairs.

Someone laughed gently.

*Yes,* Brian thought with a sigh. *Yes, someone's down there.*

He paused on the stairs, the light harsh as he blinked, trying to decide if he was doing the right thing. *Should I wait for Jenny?*

Brian knew he should, but curiosity was now getting the best of him.

He had to know what was going on.

He placed his right foot on the dirt floor and felt their presence.

A terrible chill, far worse than the one he had faced in his study. Even with the whiskey in him, Brian started to shiver as he pushed his hands deep into his pockets. He squeezed the grapeshot and started towards the hidden room. The temperature continued to drop as he crossed the floor.

The light bulb by the stairs shattered, leaving a single bulb glowing by the furnace.

Gritting his teeth Brian walked the rest of the way to enter the small room.

The false wall was still open, the air still and dark.

Brian couldn't see anything, but he heard something. Something moving in the darkness.

"Mary?" he asked, his voice hoarse and shaking.

Silence.

"Elizabeth?"

"Yes." A whisper, nothing more.

"Are you alone?" Brian asked hopefully.

"No."

His stomach plummeted. He tried to keep his breathing in check, his strained heart threatening to beat its way out of his chest.

*Christ, please don't let me die down here.*

"Who else is with you?" Brian managed to ask.

"The others."

Brian rolled his eyes and stifled a nervous chuckle. "Okay. Who are the others?"

"Mary, Nathan, Margaret. And others," Elizabeth whispered.

"Why won't Mary answer?" Brian asked.

"She can't," Elizabeth answered.

"Oh," Brian said. He took his hands out of his pockets and put them under his arms, trying not to shiver. Licking his lips nervously, he asked, "Why are you still here? Do you, do you know you're dead?"

Laughter filled the air, and not just Elizabeth's. Brian heard the deeper voices of men mingled in.

"Of course, we know we're dead," a man said. "We wish for nothing more than to be away from here."

"Do you?" a soft voice asked, and the laughter stopped.

"Do you all really wish you were no longer here?" the same soft voice asked again. "Or do you wish that you were like this man here? Flesh and blood? Spirit in the body? Able to touch and to feel, to know once more the pleasures of the body, to taste the food and to smell the autumn?"

No one answered, and Brian found that he was too afraid to even move. The cold around him was becoming unbearable. He couldn't stay in the basement much longer. He clenched his teeth tight to stop from chattering.

"They lie to you," the soft voice said. "They lie to you. If they could take your body from you, they would. Yes, they're trapped here. We all are, and there are more, far more than those buried beneath this house. The boy killed many and more. It is his passion. Yet do not think the dead wish for nothing more than freedom from this house. What you have, what you enjoy, they wish for those things as well."

"You speak too much, Edgar," a female voice hissed.

"Not enough, perhaps," Edgar replied. "You need to beware, Brian Roy. The danger to you and your wife comes not only from the boy but from some of these others as well."

A scream ripped out of the darkness, followed by dozens more and a great cacophony erupted. Fighting the urge to run in the darkness Brian made his way out of the room, heading towards the dim light showing at the top of the basement stairs.

"Where do you go my love?" a lilting voice purred in Brian's ear. "Do you not wish to stay here, to let me taste your flesh?"

A cold hand caressed the lobe of his ear.

"No," Brian said, keeping steadily on toward the stairs.

"You must," the voice said pleasantly. "You will. One night when you are with your wife, it will be me and not her. The others are not strong enough for such a thing, but I am. Look for me in your wife's eyes."

The voice's creepy happy laugh followed Brian up the stairs and sounded through the door as he slammed it closed.

## Chapter 20: Sam Starts to Read

Sam liked to read. Researching different topics was usually a relaxing way to spend an evening.

Now, though, now he was fighting the urge to read until he passed out.

Sam had gone to half a dozen libraries and as many bookstores.

On his dining table stood stacks of books. Perhaps fifty, and those were only the most reliable books that he could find on the subject of ghosts and how to remove them. Sam had no doubt that he had spoken with Paul. He had no doubt either about Paul's ability to kill and harm on a regular basis.

Sam needed a way to stop Paul. He needed to find a way to send him on to the light. More than a few of the books recommended doing that. That was how you were supposed to get rid of ghosts.

Sending the poor ghost, who wasn't aware of their own death, on to the great beyond.

Sam was fairly sure most of the advice was convoluted made up rubbish. And they were wrong about the whole not being aware 'of their own death,' thing as well.

Paul was dead. Paul knew he was dead. Paul seemed like he was having a grand old time killing things.

Sam had done a little research on deaths around the Kenyon farm.

Perhaps sixty for certain. All perfectly normal, natural deaths. Nothing unusual about it being on the farm, considering the original farm had been over three hundred acres. Three hundred acres that included thick woods, a few areas of sharp granite faced drops, a swamp, and more than a few brooks. People hunted the land when they weren't supposed to, hiked it when it was posted not to, and some had even tried to log parts of it.

In 1967, a crew of five men trying to harvest some maple trees in the northeast corner of the property died in a truck fire. All five men burned alive in the cab of the truck.

No one could figure out how five grown men had gotten into the cab of a truck, or why they had locked themselves in and didn't try to escape.

Sam had a good idea though; *Paul.*

Hunters accidentally shooting themselves. Fishermen accidentally drowning. Hikers dying from falls or medical conditions.

*Paul.*

Sam felt certain Paul had killed many and more. He was pretty sure some bodies were never found.

Sam had seen other articles in local papers over the years and never thought twice about them. Stories of men going missing on hunting trips. Hikers vanishing.

Yet while the dead included men and women, there were never any children who were killed.

Paul had always liked other children. Neither Sam nor Paul had seen many other children outside of school and yes there had been the usual fights and rivalries, but Paul had always liked the company of other kids.

Sighing, Sam closed the book he had been looking at and stood up from his chair. He walked back to the dining table, put the book down and stretched his old and tired body. Beyond the windows, the sun started its descent below the horizon, and Sam would eat a simple dinner. After that he would walk as he had always walked, regardless of Paul's threats.

Sam would walk.

Sam went into the kitchen, going about the business of getting his dinner ready and thinking about what he had read so far about ghosts.

'Going to the light,' was the one coherent theme so many of the authors had stressed. But Sam knew Paul wasn't interested in going to the light. The boy was simply having far too much fun.

The other option was to ask Paul, politely, to leave.

Sam snorted, shaking his head as he started the water to boil for the oatmeal. Again, Paul didn't want to leave.

After issuing a polite request, some of the books suggested attempting the purification of the home the ghost was attached to. But Paul was attached to the farm, and the farm was huge.

Yes, Paul's grandfather had donated some of the land, but he had donated it to the town to serve as a conservatory.

Perhaps the old man had known Paul's ghost wouldn't have been restricted to new boundaries placed upon the farm. Setting some of the land up as conservatory land would have kept people from building houses on Kenyon land. Houses where, of course, Paul would have enjoyed free reign.

So, the question was how did one go about purifying an entire farm?

It didn't sound like a feasible option.

Two options thus remained. First, Sam, and hopefully the man Brian, could find someone who might be able to exorcise Paul and send him to the afterlife whether he wanted to go or not. The second, if the first wasn't an option, was to find a way to trap Paul in one place and bind him there.

Both of those options, however, would require the assistance of Brian.

The man had seemed approachable and pleasant if a little nervous from his encounters with Paul.

Paul had been Sam's best friend. Speaking with Paul at the turnaround had been wonderful. Realizing Paul would kill him in the barn had not.

Sam sighed, brought his dinner to the table, and sat down to eat.

He would need to speak with Brian soon.

## Chapter 21: Jenny Comes Home

Brian had managed to make it back into the parlor. After turning up the heat and starting a fire in the hearth, Brian still hadn't been able to get warm until just before Jenny came home.

The click of the deadbolt caused Brian to look into the hall. He half expected to see someone other than his wife walk in.

The smile on her face fell as she looked at him. Closing the door behind her, and seeing his ashen face, Jenny asked, "Babe, are you okay?"

Brian shook his head.

"What happened... and..." Jenny paused in front of the doorway, looking down at the floor. "Is this salt on the floor?"

"Yes," Brian managed to say.

"I thought that we needed kosher sea salt," Jenny said, stepping over the line and entering the room.

"I don't know. The old man just said salt. That was it."

"What old man?" Jenny asked. She took off her coat and dropped it and her bag on the sofa before sitting down in her chair.

"The old man in the barn," Brian said, and then he told her everything that had happened. Everything about the boy and the old man all the way to the ghosts in the basement.

By the time, he was finished talking, Brian's throat hurt. Jenny sat back in her chair, her face having growing paler with each part of the story revealed.

"You can't live like this," Jenny said shortly. "We can't live like this."

"I know."

"No, I mean your heart may just give out."

"I know," Brian said. "We can't walk away from the house, though. We've put a lot into it."

"Maybe Sylvia knows someone who'd be able to help us," Jenny said. "I don't think what we need she'd be able to do herself. She seemed kind of upset about what had happened when she was here."

"Completely understandable," Brian said. His hands trembled slightly, and he knew that he wanted a drink. He didn't need one. He just wanted one.

All the more reason not to drink.

"Do you want me to ask her?" Jenny asked.

"Yes," Brian said. "I would love it if you could ask her."

A groan sounded from the hall. Brian didn't even bother looking over his shoulder. Jenny's head snapped up and she looked for the sound.

"What was that?" she asked.

"The people in the basement."

"What?"

"The dead people," Brian clarified. "The dead people in the basement. They're a little frustrated right now."

"Why?"

"Is the basement door open?" Brian asked.

Jenny shook her head. "No. Why?"

"Just making sure."

"Did you put a lock on it?"

"Sort of."

"What do you mean 'sort of'?"

"I took the hammer and some four-inch nails and nailed the damned thing shut."

"Oh."

Brian nervously switched the grapeshot from his right hand to his left.

"Did you try salt?" she asked.

"Yup."

"Did it work?"

"Nope. Evidently the little bastards can still open a door, evidently just not cross the line."

"What's that groaning sound?" Jenny asked.

Brian looked at her tiredly. "The sound of dead people pushing the nails back out. They'll have the door open soon."

The groan sounded again, ending sharply before being followed closely by a loud clatter.

"That was the second nail," Brian said, with just a hint of pride. "Only eight more to go," he shouted at the ghosts behind the door. Laughter chased his words and something heavy banged against the basement door.

## Chapter 22: Sam Risks the Kenyon Farm

A soft snow fell from the sky, the clouds hiding the moon and the stars. Sam's small flashlight reflected brilliantly in the snowflakes and the light layer of snow coating Old Nashua Road. At the intersection, he paused, waiting for a plow with its blades up to pass before turning around and heading back the way he had come. The driver gave a quick pull on its air-horn.

It was probably one of the few men working for the State that Sam had known.

Sam waved at the disappearing lights of the truck, the spreader on the back of the mammoth vehicle spinning and throwing out a wide arc of salt and sand on the pavement. Walking at an easy, careful pace Sam aimed towards his house, which he knew he would eventually pass by on his way to the turnaround.

He started to wonder why, after so many years, did Paul speak with him? Was it because Brian and his wife had moved into the Kenyon house? But that really couldn't be it. Others had lived in the house, tenants, none of whom stayed longer than necessary. With so few houses on the road it was easy to know who came and who went. Who stayed and who didn't.

Never had someone other than a Kenyon owned the home, though.

Was the loss of the home part of the answer; the fact that someone other than a Kenyon now owned the property?

Part of Sam wanted to say yes, but he knew new owners couldn't be the sole reason.

Paul had enjoyed killing long before someone new moved in, that much was now obvious.

No, Brian may have helped irritate Paul, but he wasn't the sole responsible person. In fact, Brian wasn't responsible at all.

Paul was a rotten kid. Far more rotten than Sam had ever known.

Sam passed by his house, the front light shining brightly on the porch, the lamp in his dining room glowing warmly. Soon he would be in the warmth of his own home, but first he wanted to stop at Brian's house.

Sam needed to speak with the man.

Taking his pipe out of his coat pocket, Sam paused long enough to relight the tobacco before continuing on with his walk. The familiar, pleasant smell of his pipe mingled with the smell of the snow.

Snowflakes hissed as they struck the embers, his own footsteps muffled by the snow falling. The snowfall was still light, but it was slowly building in intensity

Sam remembered the many snowstorms he had worked, both as the driver of a plow and as a foreman. Part of him missed the work; the older part of him did not.

He caught sight of the Kenyon house.

All of the lights on the first floor were on. Two cars were in the driveway, each of them with a light coating of snow. Sam had started his walk far later than usual, and if the wind was right, even with the deadening effects of the snow, he would hear the bell at the First Congregationalist Church chime eight o'clock.

Feeling anxious Sam passed by the house, reached the turnaround and looked nervously for Paul.

Sam couldn't see his old friend anywhere.

He felt no relief, however. Part of him was sure that Paul was watching him, waiting for him to come too close.

Taking a long pull off of his pipe, Sam let the smoke out and crossed the road. He walked back along the now snow covered asphalt, his own footprints rapidly disappearing as the snow continued to fall. In a moment, he stopped at the driveway of the Kenyon house.

*No need to wait on what you know needs to be done,* Sam thought.

Straightening up, he walked the length of the driveway, held the railing with a gloved hand and climbed the stairs to the porch. He rang the bell and waited.

A moment later the door opened, and a pretty woman answered the door.

"Yes?" she asked, her eyes flicking past him, instantly registering his lack of a car.

Sam took the pipe out of his mouth and smiled at her. He liked this woman already. "My name is Samuel Hall."

Her smile pleasantly interrupted him. "Mr. Hall. Yes, Brian mentioned that he saw you today. You didn't come back, though."

"I did not," Sam admitted guiltily.

"Well, if you like you can come in," she said, stepping aside and holding the door open.

"Thank you," Sam said. He went to put his pipe down on the porch railing, and she stopped him.

"Don't worry about that," she laughed. "Thank you, though. Brian's having a cigar right now."

"Thank you," Sam smiled. Putting the pipe stem back into his mouth Sam walked into the house, the woman closing the door behind him.

"I'm Jenny, by the way," she said, locking the door.

"Sam," Sam responded. He pulled off a glove and shook her hand. "A pleasure."

"Likewise. You can just put your things on the boot tray if you like, and there's a hook on the back of the door for your jacket."

Jenny waited as he shed his winter gear, even stepping out of his boots. He could remember Paul's mother always insisting that the boys do that, regardless of the season or the door that they entered through. She had not kept the rooms clean for little boys to make dirty.

Straightening up, Sam glanced at the basement door and stopped.

A hammer lay on its side by the door, long, four-inch nails scattered on the floor. The door was open a few inches, and he could see the holes in the door where the nails had been driven through.

"Brian tried to make sure the door stayed closed," Jenny said.

Sam followed her into the parlor, careful to mind the layer of salt on the threshold.

Brian was sitting in the same chair that he had been in earlier, and the man looked ill-used. Brian raised an eyebrow as Sam sat down on the sofa. Jenny sat down in a chair across from her husband.

"I am glad to see you," Brian said after a moment. "I honestly expected to find you dead in the barn the next time I gathered up the courage to go out there."

Sam nodded. "It was an unpleasant experience. I saw Paul out there. Had we not been friends in our childhood I think that he would have killed me."

"But yet here you are again," Brian said. "Why?"

"Paul has to be sent on his way," Sam said. "More than likely his grandfather is still here because of Paul as well. At first, I thought Paul was being kept here by his grandfather, but I think the man is here to keep Paul from others. If Paul can be sent on then, perhaps the grandfather can as well."

"There's more than just the grandfather and the boy," Jenny said.

Sam frowned. "What do you mean?"

"There are more ghosts, more dead people," Brian said tiredly. "In the basement there are graves, Kenyon family one and all. And it's not just the dead family members kicking around. Oh no. There's a whole congress of the dead bastards. There are nine that we're sure of, but after that, well, who knows. Our friend said that there were a lot more hanging out on the edges."

"On the edges," Sam said, "like where they were killed."

"What?" Jenny asked.

"Over the decades," Sam said, taking his pipe out of his mouth, "there have been many deaths associated with the Kenyon property. Most people don't realize or remember just how big the farm used to be. Until the seventies, the property belonged solely to Paul's grandfather, Mr. Richard W. Kenyon. Shortly before his death, however, he deeded the lion's share of his land to the town, to be kept as conservation land. More than two hundred acres."

"Damn," Jenny said.

Brian nodded his agreement.

"With a property as vast as the Kenyons', and with one covering everything from swamps to forest, there are plenty of opportunities for someone to become injured," Sam continued.

"And a lot of people were injured," Jenny said, closing her eyes. "We're pretty sure that a lot of them were out and killed.

71

Our friend Sylvia said the same the other night. She said there were others on the periphery, watching, waiting to see what happened. People trapped but unable to leave. They're held here by something, she just couldn't figure out what."

"She's a perceptive woman," Sam said.

"She is," Brian agreed. "More than I gave her credit for."

"So," Jenny said. "How do we go about sending all of these ghosts on their way?"

"I've done a little research," Sam said. "Just a little, mind you. There's a lot of information out there and really no way to tell the good from the bad. It looks as though an exorcism could be tried. We don't want to try and simply cast them out of the house, or from the property. That could set them loose on other people."

"What if an exorcism doesn't work?" Brian asked, sitting up a little in his chair. "Is there another option other than casting them out of the house?"

"I have read that there are ways to trap ghosts," Sam said. "I do not, however, have any experience in such matters."

"Sylvia does," Jenny said.

"Will she come back?" Brian asked.

Jenny shrugged. "I don't know. I'll ask her. She might even be able to bring someone else to help, or to take care of it all together."

"And what if we don't want to go?" a low voice asked.

Sam looked to the doorway and saw a large ghost standing there. The specter was that of a man, nearly filling the doorway. His form slid in and out of the world, yet Sam realized he had seen the man before. Stern photographs in the house when Paul had still lived.

*One of Paul's relatives.* An old Civil War veteran. A man of pure violence, if the oral history of Paul's family had been true.

Sam believed the stories.

The ghost looked malignant.

"I don't want to go," the man said, looking down smugly at the salt. "There are many of us who don't want to go, bound as we are to this place. I have many and more things that I wish to do to those who travel my lands."

Brian looked at the ghost and then turned his back to it.

"Anyway," Brian said with a sigh. He took a long pull off of his cigar and looked at Sam. "You think that someone can actually trap them if they can't be exorcised and we can't be bad neighbors and just kick the ghosts out?"

"Yes," Sam said.

"I'll send Sylvia a text now," Jenny said, picking her phone up off of the coffee table.

A strange, surprisingly comfortable silence fell over the room.

Until the ghost spoke again.

"Do you really think that you can remove us from our home?" the ghost asked, chuckling. "You cannot."

Sam watched Brian get up, transfer something from his left hand to his right and walk to the doorway.

Brian took his cigar out of his mouth, exhaled and as he put the cigar back he threw a punch with his right hand.

The ghost laughed, but the laugh turned instantly into a howl of rage as Brian's fist passed through the ghost.

"Prick," Brian said, walking back to his chair.

"How the hell did you do that?" Jenny asked, voicing Sam's own question.

Sitting down Brian opened his right hand and showed them the small iron ball he had been holding. "Iron. Just like Sylvia, and Paul's grandfather said. Iron."

Jenny's phone chimed, and she picked it up.

"Sylvia said she doesn't do anything like that, but she has a friend who does. She gave him our information and he's on his way," Jenny said.

"Good," Brian said grimly. "Anybody want some coffee or something to drink?"

"Coffee please, babe," Jenny smiled.

"Water please," Sam said. A feeling of nervous excitement raced through him as he thought about someone coming to deal with the ghosts.

"Two coffees and one water," Brian said, standing up again. "Let's hope none of the dead get annoyed because I'm in the kitchen."

Sam watched as Brian left the room, the muscles of the man's jaw seeming to dance under the skin.

# Moving In

*He's more afraid than he's letting on,* Sam thought. *But he sure does seem as angry as he does scared. He's a good man.*

Silence settled over the room as he and Jenny waited for their drinks, the logs in the fireplace snapping behind them. Somewhere in the house, a person laughed, and footsteps ran across the floor above them.

"I hope Sylvia's friend gets here soon," Jenny said, a note of anxiety in her otherwise calm voice. She pulled at an earlobe and tapped her foot.

Sam could only nod in agreement.

## Chapter 23: Leo Moreland Arrives

Leo surrounded himself with books.

Literally.

His two room apartment was a massive gathering of books.

The books, most of them careworn and well-read, were written in an array of languages. They were also piled on everything except the coffee maker, and Leo's bed.

His bathroom didn't have any books in it though. Leo feared for their safety around water.

Leo had four pieces of furniture. A desk for research, an old Queen Anne, wingback chair battered by time, the narrow bunk he slept on, and the bureau for his clothes.

Few people were allowed into his apartment.

The windows were covered by bookshelves. The sun damaged books.

Leo had two lights. One behind his chair and one on the desk. He didn't trust electricity, and he made sure everything was unplugged before he went to bed and when he left the house. He had his reasons.

Leo hated the very idea of fire near his books. So he didn't have a kitchen. He didn't have a microwave. Just a coffee maker.

Leo ate out for every meal. Leo ate every meal at the small restaurant in the building across from his own.

He made good money doing research for people, writing for people, and trapping ghosts.

Leo disliked trapping ghosts, but it was something he knew had to be done.

When Leo trapped a ghost, he bound it within a miniature edition of Shakespeare's *Macbeth*. He would bring the book to a medium who could then take the necessary time to convince the ghost to move on.

Leo made good money: Money to pay for his apartment, money to pay for his meals, and most importantly money to pay for his books.

Leo was sitting on his bed, taking his shoes off when his phone buzzed.

He picked it up off of the floor. The text was from Sylvia.

*Can you help a friend of mine and her husband?*
*Yes*, he sent back.
*Thank you.*
A moment later an address in Mont Vernon followed.
*It's bad*, she added.
*Okay.*

Leo put his shoes back on, wondering how much a cab to Mont Vernon would cost. He picked up his phone and called the cab company, requested Frank and gave the address.

"It's going to be an hour or so before he gets there," the dispatcher said.

"This is Leo."

"Leo?" the dispatcher asked and in the background, Leo heard someone speak. "Oh. Um, Frank's on his way. About five minutes."

"Thank you."

*New dispatcher*, Leo thought. *Everyone else knows my voice.*

Leo took his wallet and keys off of the desk, as well as his miniature *Macbeth*. He took his jacket off of the back of his chair and pulled it on before unplugging the electrical cords.

Soon he was standing at the entrance of the building, slightly out of the snowfall which increased steadily as he waited. Within several minutes, a maroon Mercury Sable with 'SK Taxi Service' on the sides pulled up.

Leo stepped out into the weather, hunching his shoulders against the snow as he crossed the old sidewalk to the car. Leo opened the back passenger side door and climbed in.

"Hello, Leo," Frank said, smiling at him in the rearview mirror.

Leo smiled back. "Hello, Frank."

"Mont Vernon?"

"Yes. How much?"

"Twenty for you, Leo," Frank said, not bothering to signal as he shifted gear and pulled away from the curb. "Need me to wait when I get you there?"

"Please."

Leo buckled up as Frank picked up speed, disregarding and ignoring road signs, most traffic lights and the weather in general.

Leo forced himself to relax. Frank had been his preferred driver for nearly ten years now. Frank's first cab had been haunted, and Leo had helped the ghost move on. The ghost, an irritated Unitarian minister, had caused several minor accidents by disturbing the other cab's electrical systems.

Frank had never forgotten what Leo had done. Thus, Leo had a nearly guaranteed ride whenever he happened to need one. Which wasn't particularly often, but it was still nice to know it was there when he needed it.

It meant less time to worry, and more time to read and research.

The ride to Mont Vernon took nearly half an hour even with Frank's cavalier attitude towards the rules of the road. Frank also filled Leo in on the state of his love life, the ongoing battle with his second ex-wife over their son, his first ex-wife and her alimony payments, and the need for him to move because his landlady expected regular conjugal visits if he was going to be late with the rent.

Frank had also stopped the cab once so he could get an extra-large coffee at Dunkin Donuts. Leo took medium hot black, his staple beverage outside of water.

Leo was only half way through the coffee when they turned onto Old Nashua Road and made their way to the house of Sylvia's friends. When they reached it, Leo could see the lights on and two snow covered cars in the driveway.

The dead were everywhere.

Dozens of them. All around the house and on the house's side of the road.

"Pull over to the right, please," Leo said.

Frank did so without asking why.

Once the cab stopped, Leo said, "Please stay on this side of the road, Frank. Do not walk over to the house, or even park on the other side. Stay here. I will walk back out to you. I don't want you to have anything to do with this house, okay?"

Frank's eyes had widened slightly, but the normally talkative man merely nodded in silence.

"I'll come out in an hour and a half to let you know what's going on," Leo continued. He took out his wallet and fished out a trio of twenties. "Here. This is for the ride here and the time you'll have to wait. If I'm not out at ten o'clock, you leave. Do not come in after me."

Frank took the money, and nodded.

Leo smiled. "I will see you soon, Frank."

"I hope so," Frank said quietly when Leo could no longer hear him. "I hope so."

Leo turned his collar up against the cold, and walked across the road. The dead turned to look at him, and Leo ignored them. He didn't want them knowing just yet that he could see them. That would come in good time, and he was certain that it would be irritating to them.

The dead liked to look, but they didn't like to be seen.

Leo walked up the driveway, making fresh tracks in the snow as he advanced upon the house. Shapes appeared and disappeared in the corners of his eyes, and he sighed. He couldn't even count how many were around the house, let alone how many would be in the house. He had a feeling he would find far too many for his liking.

Most of the trapping would have to be done tonight. The other ghosts would get wise and hide, but he would find them.

*But how to go about trapping them all?* he asked himself. *There are so many.*

Leo climbed the porch steps, past a rather depressed looking ghost dressed as a hunter, and rang the bell.

A moment later a man answered the door. He was probably Leo's own age, but he looked exhausted. Careworn. As though something had gone terribly wrong.

*Well,* Leo thought. *For most people it has.*

"Hello," Leo said, giving the man a small smile. "My name is Leo. Sylvia asked me to come."

"Hi Leo," the man said, extending his hand. "I'm Brian."

Leo forced himself to quickly shake Brian's hand. His nose wrinkled. "You're carrying iron."

Brian's eyes widened in surprise as he nodded.

"Good," Leo said. "May I come in?"

"Uh, yeah, come on in."

78

Leo stepped into the house, saw a young girl at an open door, peering out at him. The holes in the door and the hammer and nails on the floor suggested that the door wouldn't stay shut.

Leo pretended that he hadn't seen the girl and continued to look. Down the hall, he saw an older woman standing in another doorway, and to the right, there was a line of salt across the floor.

Leo walked to that room as Brian closed and locked the door behind him.

When Leo stepped into the protected room, he saw an old man sitting on a sofa and a woman who had to be Sylvia's friend, sitting in a chair beside the larger piece of furniture. The man, Leo saw, had a black pall around him.

The man was dying. Leo wasn't sure if the man knew it or not.

A narrow, ladder-back chair with a rush seat stood against the wall facing the others, and Leo sat down in it. Brian took a seat, and the three people looked at Leo.

Leo gave them all his small smile.

"My name is Leo," he said. "I have been asked by Sylvia to help you. What is it that you want?"

"We have some ghosts here," the woman said. "We want them gone."

"Exorcised if we can," the old man said. "Trapped if we can't."

Leo nodded.

"You can do this?" Brian asked.

"Yes."

"How much would it cost?" Brian asked.

"Sylvia asked me to do it," Leo said. "It won't cost anything."

"What do you normally get?" the woman asked.

"One thousand dollars per ghost."

"There's more than one here," the old man said. "And they're none too pleasant, for the most part."

"Much more than one," Leo said, nodding in agreement.

"How many more?" Brian asked.

"I counted, at least, thirty-seven in the front yard," Leo said. "One looking out from the door in the hall, another from the kitchen."

Someone went running upstairs. The other three looked up, but Leo did not.

"I assume there are more," Leo continued. "Is there a barn?"

"Left side of the property," the old man said, looking back to Leo.

"There will be more there."

"What do you think will work?" the woman asked.

"No exorcism," Leo said promptly. "Too many. You would never get them all. Maybe, if we can trap most of them, an exorcism would work."

"How are you going to trap them?" Brian asked. "I mean, not to sound stupid, but the only the only time that I ever saw ghosts being trapped was in Ghostbusters."

Leo nodded. "You have to catch them. You have to bind them to an object. From there you find a medium who might be able to work with the dead. Or you bind them to something else that they won't break free from."

"How do you catch them?" the old man asked. "From what I've gathered, they only announce themselves when they feel good and ready to."

"Yes," Leo said, nodding. "You have to see them to catch them."

"If there's more than one," the woman said, "won't they stay hidden once they realize what it is you're doing?"

"Yes."

"Okay," Brian said, shaking his head. "How do you catch them when they don't want to be seen?"

"That doesn't matter to me," Leo said.

"Why?" the old man asked.

Leo looked at him. "I see the dead whether they wish to be seen or not."

## Chapter 24: The Ghost Trapper

Brian blinked several times.

"I'm sorry," Brian said after a moment. "Did you say that you can see them even when they don't want to be seen?"

The curious little man named Leo nodded. The man's pale face was narrow and he looked absurdly small in his jacket, his black pants rumpled and his brown hair cut extremely close. The man was strange, perhaps with some form of high functioning autism.

Brian almost didn't believe the man's assertion about seeing the dead, but then again, Brian had seen some incredibly disturbing things over the past few days.

If Leo could help, then more power to him.

"You see the dead," Sam said softly.

Leo looked at the man as if the single nod had been enough of a response regardless as to how many times the statement might be made.

"How long will it take?" Jenny asked, ever the pragmatist.

Leo shrugged. "It depends on a variety of factors. I must operate on the assumption that all of the ghosts will inevitably have been drawn to either this building or the barn. If there is another structure on the property, then that will have to be examined as well. Graveyards on the property too."

"Can you start tonight?" Jenny asked.

"Yes." Leo stood up. "I must leave here at ten. I must be back in Nashua by midnight."

Brian stifled the urge to ask if he was going to turn back into a scullery maid, but he thought the Cinderella reference might be beyond Leo's ability to grasp.

"You are more than welcome to attend," Leo said, walking out of the parlor.

Brian looked to Jenny and to Sam, and both of them shrugged. Together the three of them left the parlor, stopping in the hallway as Leo squatted down in front of the partially open basement door.

For the first time, Leo gave a relaxed and genuine smile. From an inner pocket, he produced a small, red leather book the size of a matchbox.

"Hello," Leo said softly. "What's your name?"

There was a pause as Leo listened for a response. His smile broadened, and Leo said, "Isabella. Isabella, that's a beautiful name. My name is Leonidas, but I would be pleased if you would call me Leo."

"Yes," Leo said after a moment. "I am going to ask you a question, Isabella. Do you want to leave here?"

"Very good," Leo smiled. He opened the small book, whispered a word that Brian didn't quite catch, and then he closed the book. A moment later he stood up, closing the door to the basement quietly. He looked at Brian and Jenny and Sam. "She said to watch out for Henry, and someone named Paul."

"We know about Paul," Jenny said. "But who is Henry?"

"Someone bad," Leo said. "Someone bad."

*Great,* Brian thought.

They followed him into the kitchen where Leo came to a stop in the center of the room.

"Hello," Leo said, looking at the refrigerator. "Ah. I'm sorry. Do you understand me, though?"

Leo frowned, and then he nodded. "Yes. Yes, I understand."

"Oh," Leo said, glancing over to the left. "Mary. Mary, do you want to leave here?"

A glass came hurtling through the kitchen, shattering against the far cabinet.

"Shit!" Brian said, stumbling back, Jenny catching him as his heart seemed to ricochet in his chest. Sam helped her get Brian into a chair.

Leo did nothing more than look at where the glass had come from and Brian caught sight of a tight, angry smile on the small man's face.

## Chapter 25: Introducing Henry

Leo looked at the same angry man he had seen standing outside of the parlor.

"Hello Henry," Leo said.

A look of surprise flickered over the dead man's face.

Mary and Elizabeth slipped away to a far corner of the kitchen while Brian and the others gathered at the table.

"Yes," Leo said, still looking at Henry. "Yes, I can see you."

Henry said nothing as if not quite believing what Leo said.

"Come closer, Henry," Leo said softly.

The ghost took an involuntary step forward, a look of horror on his face.

"Come now," Leo said in the same soft voice, "closer still, Henry. Closer still."

"No," Henry hissed. Yet he took another step towards Leo. "How?!"

"Long hours alone with books," Leo answered. "Long hours alone with the likes of you. Strange things will happen to a boy."

"Leave me be," Henry snarled.

Leo gestured with his left hand, and Henry jerked forward as though he were a fish on a line, trying to fight, pulling back.

Leo had taken far worse than someone as disagreeable as Henry, though perhaps not as evil in their intent. Leo opened up *Macbeth* and fear seemed to glisten in the ghost's eyes. Leo felt a warm rush of satisfaction.

Carefully Leo reeled Henry in. As pleased as he was with himself Leo knew that the slightest sign of weakness could shatter the effort, proving it all the more difficult to bind the ghost to the book. Leo focused on Henry, pulling the ghost in, ignoring the screams, then the curses, and finally the pleas.

Leo ignored them all.

With sheer will, he forced Henry into the book and closed it.

When he turned around Leo was not surprised to see that both Elizabeth and Mary had disappeared. It would take some time to get them back and into the book.

He would have to convince them that it was okay, that the book served simply as a focal point for a door, an entry into a world which was as pleasant or as horrible as the trapped ghost made it. For each soul it was different. To Leo it mattered not.

Blinking his eyes Leo looked at Brian and Jenny, and the walking dead man who probably still didn't know.

"Are you well?" Leo asked Brian.

Brian nodded.

"Perhaps you should remain in the kitchen," Leo said. "I will, with your permission, go through the house. I have forty-eight minutes until I must leave your house and return to Nashua. I believe that I will be able to induce more than a few to enter the book before I must leave."

"Sounds good to me," Brian said with a pained grin.

Leo nodded, turned his back on the trio in the kitchen and made his way back to the hallway. He stopped right outside the basement door and listened. Upstairs he heard footsteps, people talking. Below him came the sound of muffled voices. There would be some in the attic as well. There were always some in the attic. He disliked the cliché. Ghosts were somehow so predictable sometimes. He would have to check for servants' stairs and servants' quarters, closets and pantries, root cellars, and of course, the barn. Leo would have to ask if there were other structures on the property, aside from the graveyard he had already been told about under the house.

*But I will begin with the attic,* Leo thought. Forcing himself to focus he repeated aloud, "But I will begin with the attic."

He started up the stairs, his book in his hand.

*Yes, I will start in the attic and work my way down.*

Nearing the top of the stairs he saw someone dash into a shadow just ahead of him.

*I must not get carried away,* he told himself. *I must not forget what must not be forgotten.*

*I have forty-six minutes left before I must leave the house. Then I must cross the yard. And then I must cross the street, I must cross the street and get into Frank's cab and return home.*

*I must not delay.*

# Moving In

*I must not delay.*

## Chapter 26: Frank Figueroa Makes a Mistake

At nine thirty, Frank got out of his cab, cleaned the snow off of the car and was thankful that for once his cell phone service was terrible. Neither his first ex-wife nor the second had been able to get a hold of him. He hadn't even been able to talk to his current wife, but then, by nine-thirty she was usually too drunk to be understood anyway.

Finishing up with the car Frank slapped his hands together, getting the last bit of snow off his gloves, and climbed back into the cab. He started the car up to let it run for a little while, just enough to take an edge off of the cold New Hampshire night air. He didn't mind the cold in little doses, and he wanted to make sure that Leo would be okay. The guy was strange, but he had a good heart. Frank wanted to make sure that nothing happened to him.

Frank turned on the radio, then grunted and turned it off as the announcer said that the Celtics were down by twelve to the Knicks.

"They suck," Frank muttered. He draped his arms over the steering wheel, then rested his head on his forearms.

He still had half an hour until the little man came out and they could head back to Nashua. But his bladder wouldn't wait that long. He'd have to get out into the cold to relieve himself.

Frank hated going to the bathroom outside. He had promised himself after his time in the army that he wouldn't ever go to the bathroom outside again; a promise broken multiple times in the past thirty years, but it was still a promise that he hated breaking. Besides, he really didn't enjoy exposing his privates to the New Hampshire winter.

Frank jerked his head up, looking out his door window. Something had made a sudden sharp noise. But he didn't see anything through the windows. The snow had started clinging to the glass again.

Grumbling, Frank rolled the window down and looked out at the house.

A small shape, dashed around the front of one of the cars in the driveway and the sound of glass shattering ripped through the night's stillness.

"What the hell?" Frank said. He put the window up and got out of the car, leaving it running with the heat blasting.

Another smashing sound exploded into the cold air and Frank crossed the road.

Frank walked with a purpose. Thirty years ago he had been a young military policeman. His body remembered everything. Within a few steps, his back had straightened, his shoulders were squared, and his stride was long and steady, his arms swinging in perfect rhythm with his walk.

Frank forgot though that he was fifty-two and had a two-pack a day habit. He also forgot that he was seventy pounds heavier than he had been when he was twenty-one.

All Frank knew was someone was breaking the windows of the cars at the house where Leo was. That someone looked like a child. First, the child shouldn't be out so late in the snow. Second, the child sure as hell shouldn't be breaking windows.

Ignorant of the snow landing on his face and melting against his skin, Frank reached the driveway.

A boy, maybe ten or eleven, maybe a little older, stepped out from behind one of the cars. He smiled and waved at Frank.

"Hello!" the boy said, his voice cheerful as he walked towards Frank.

"Hey," Frank said, coming to a stop. "Are you breaking windows?"

"Yes," the boy said, nodding. "Yes, I certainly am."

"What?" Frank asked. "Why?"

"Because I wanted you to come over here." the boy said, stopping a few feet away from Frank.

"Why?" Frank said, feeling confused. Fear started to ripple through him as he remembered that Leo hadn't wanted him to cross the road.

Leo had wanted him to stay with the car. Frank took a cautious step back.

The smile on the boy's face seemed to get bigger

"Don't walk away," the strange boy said softly, taking a step closer. "I need you to send a message to my friends inside."

Frank swallowed nervously. He should have stayed in the car. There was something wrong with the boy. Something terribly wrong.

"What message?" Frank managed to ask.

"I'll tell you," the boy whispered, and he stepped forward, hand outstretched.

When the boy's hand touched Frank's arm, a terrible, biting cold raced through him, and Frank struggled not to scream.

Just as Frank took his last breath, the boy leaned in close so that he could whisper in Frank's ear.

"This is my message," Paul hissed.

## Chapter 27: Paul's Message to his Friends

In the parlor, Brian sat beside Jenny on the sofa and Sam sat on the ladder-back chair. The fire he had started in the hearth was just beginning to throw warmth out into the room. They could hear Leo now moving around on the second floor having finished with the attic.

There had been yelling, and things crashing. Brian had even heard the sound of breaking glass from both the attic and from outside.

None of them wanted to disturb the curious man as he worked, and, quite frankly, since Brian couldn't see any of the ghosts when they didn't want to be seen, he really didn't want to be in striking distance if one of them got upset and lashed out in his direction.

Brian had enough of such things when the light exploded in his office earlier.

For the first time since they had moved out of the city, he took out his bottle of nitroglycerine pills and popped one into his mouth.

"Are you okay?" Jenny asked.

Brian shook his head. "No. This place is really stressing me out."

"We'll pack some stuff up once he's done then," Jenny said, "and we'll stay at my mom's for a couple of days. Let Leo do his thing."

"Sounds good."

"What's wrong?" Sam asked.

"Bad ticker," Brian said, tapping his chest. "I've had two heart attacks already. My doctor is pretty sure that the third will do me in."

"I'm sorry to hear that."

Brian opened his mouth to reply when a heavy knock on the front door cut him off.

The three of them looked in unison out into the hallway.

Another knock followed, heavier and harder than the first. It was quickly followed by a third, and then a fourth, each of them stronger than the last. The entire house seemed to shake as the pounding continued.

Brian stood up, worked his jaw nervously and walked to the doorway of the parlor, staying just behind the line of salt. He looked at the front door and watched it shake in its frame with each blow.

The noise ceased suddenly. There was a thump on the porch.

Brian stepped out of the parlor.

"Babe," Jenny said. "Where are you going?"

"I think something's on the porch," he answered.

"Hold on," she said.

Brian stood in the hallway and glanced over as Jenny and Sam came out into the hall with him. Brian walked to the front door and opened it.

A man's body lay on the floor, twisted in the curious way that let Brian know the man wasn't sleeping or passed out. There was no way to mistake it, especially since the man's head was nothing more than a bloody pulp with yellowish bone and gray brain exposed to the world.

At the bottom of the stairs, outside in the snow, however, stood Paul Kenyon.

He was smiling proudly, like a cat having delivered a dead bird for the family.

"Hello, Sam!" Paul said, his voice cheerful. "I'm still here, you know."

"I know," Sam said in a low voice.

"And Brian," Paul grinned. "You pulled a pretty neat trick with that chain. I did not see that coming. And is that your wife; is that Jenny? She's pretty, Brian."

Jenny said nothing as she slipped her hand into Brian's and squeezed.

"You're – you're all here," Paul said. "But there's a stranger in my house, and he's taking my friends and family away."

Paul's demeanor suddenly changed, and Jenny shivered as she saw the evil innocence in his eyes.

"You bring Leonidas Moreland outside to me," Paul snapped. "Take his damned little book away from him, too. If you don't, I'll make you miserable. You'll never leave this place. You'll starve to death, slow and steady."

Suddenly Paul smiled. "Of course, then you'll get to stay with me forever. And that will be so much fun. Either way, Leonidas Moreland dies."

Silence fell over all of them. Brian could hear the snowflakes falling in the silence that followed.

Paul suddenly smiled again. "Bring him soon!" And then he skipped away laughing into the night.

Brian sighed, closed the door and walked back to the parlor. He sat down in his own chair while Jenny went to her chair and Sam sat down on the sofa.

Sam took out his pipe and his tobacco pouch. Brian watched the man pack the pipe, light it, and sit back, staring at the hallway.

After a moment, Sam let out a long stream of smoke, watched it curl up towards the tin ceiling. "I don't know about you, but I'm not overly keen on that little boy anymore," he said.

Brian and Jenny could only nod their agreement.

## Chapter 28: Leo on the Second Floor

Leo had just managed to talk a frightened middle-aged hiker into the book when he heard a rustling behind him.

"Leo," a very familiar voice said.

Leo straightened up and turned around. *No, not you.*

It was Frank.

"I'm sorry, Leo," Frank said.

"So am I," Leo said. He gave Frank a small smile. "This is what I was concerned about. You should have stayed in the cab."

Frank shrugged. "Did you hear the banging downstairs?"

Leo shook his head.

"Of course not," Frank chuckled. "A kid got me, can you believe that, Leo, a kid. He also told them downstairs that he wants you to come out. He sent me up here to tell you the same thing."

"I am not surprised. Will you enter the book, Frank?"

Leo opened *Macbeth* and looked at the taxi driver.

Frank nodded. "See you around, Leo."

"Goodbye, Frank."

Frank slipped away into mist and Leo closed the book. More ghosts waited on the second floor, but the boy needed to be dealt with.

Pocketing the book, Leo left the room and made his way downstairs. He found Brian, the woman, and the older man standing in the hallway by the front door. All three of them looked dazed and slightly shocked.

Brian looked over at Leo.

"There's a body on the porch," Brian said.

"I know," Leo said, stopping at the bottom of the stairs. "That was my taxi driver, Frank. He told me what happened. Apparently, the boy, Paul wants to see me."

"He's dangerous," Sam warned.

"Of course, he is," Leo responded. "But Paul is not the worst of them."

"Are you serious?" said Jenny.

"Of course," Leo said. "Excuse me, it would be rude to keep him waiting."

The trio moved away from the door, to let the strange little man pass.

Leo went to the door, opened it and stepped outside. He ignored Frank's remains, and looked around the yard and saw the boy standing beneath a tree.

"Hello," Leo said, walking down the stairs.

"Hi!" Paul waved. He walked towards Leo. "I'm so happy you came outside like you were asked."

"So am I," Leo said. "Why did you wish to see me?"

"I've never met anyone that can see me when I don't want to be seen," the boy said, looking at Leo. "Are there many like you?"

Leo shrugged. "I really couldn't say. I don't speak with the living very often."

"They're not very nice. Especially grown-ups."

"What do you have to say?" Leo asked.

"That you need to leave," Paul warned coldly.

"I won't," Leo said.

"Good," the boy laughed. "This is going to be so much fun. I normally make my grandfather run everywhere. He tries to stop me from having fun."

"He doesn't like your fun," Leo said, glancing over the boy's shoulder. Paul's grandfather stood watching, marking his sad vigil.

"Nope."

"Is that why he's watching you now?" Leo asked.

The boy turned around and waved.

"Yes," the boy said, turning back to Leo. "He's worried that I'm going to hurt you."

"You could always try."

"I want to," the boy said with a sigh, "but the big chief wants to see you, so I really can't."

"Will you bring me to your 'big chief?'"

Paul nodded.

Leo turned and looked at the others who still stood in the doorway, watching. "I'll be back. Close the door and seal yourselves in."

In the cold, still air, Leo could hear it click shut.

# Moving In

In his mind, Leo heard the ticking of a clock. It wasn't a real clock, but one in his head. Just a simple alarm clock like his grandmother had once had, a folding alarm clock that could be tucked away in a green leather case. A clock that reminded him of midnight's approach.

He wouldn't be home.

He wouldn't be home.

Tonight would not end well.

He had little more than two hours to finish the job.

"Lead the way, please," Leo said. "I will follow."

## Chapter 29: Under Attack

When Brian locked the door, Jenny and Sam walked back to the parlor. Brian followed a moment later and put another log on the fire. Outside the wind picked up, rattling the window in its frame, and a glance out of it showed the snowfall was heavier.

A storm was coming.

Brian hoped it wasn't some sort of omen.

Brian's stomach rumbled unpleasantly and clenched, and he realized he hadn't eaten since breakfast. "I'm going to grab something to eat, anyone else hungry?"

Both Jenny and Sam shook their heads.

"Babe," Jenny said, "shouldn't you stay in here? Leo didn't want us leaving the parlor."

"I'll be okay. It's our house. Anyway, I'll be right back," Brian said. He left the parlor, eyeing the basement door nervously but feeling a little better since Leo had been working his tricks in the house. Brian wondered how many of the ghosts the man had managed to convince to leave.

*Hopefully all of them,* he thought.

He reached the kitchen, avoided the shards of broken glass which would have to be cleaned up later, and went to the pantry. The pantry was huge, bigger than some walk-in closets that Brian had seen. He and Jenny hadn't really been able to stock it to their liking, but there was some food in it, including the protein bars that he and Jenny enjoyed eating.

Turning on the light, Brian pulled a bar out, opened it and -

The door slammed closed.

The bulb suddenly shattered and Brian was plunged into darkness.

Something slammed into Brian, thrusting him back into the shelves. He grunted, pain exploding in his back. Blows landed against his head, vicious, horrific strikes that left his ears ringing.

Brian stumbled a step forward and was shoved from behind, bouncing him off the shelves across from him. He fell to his knees and an involuntary scream ripped out of his mouth as shards of the broken bulb cut through his pants, digging deep into his skin.

Frantically Brian thrust his hand into his pocket, getting a grip on the grapeshot when another blow landed squarely on his forehead. Even in the darkness stars exploded in front of his eyes and he went over to his side.

Something struck his groin, pain exploding in his abdomen and he threw up the coffee he had earlier. His mouth burned from the bile and with his heart beating erratically Brian finally managed to pull the grapeshot out. Desperately he swung his arm, hoping that his fist would connect with something. Anything.

A hiss came from his left and Brian swung that way.

Pushing himself to his knees Brian heard the hiss again, this time to his right and he tensed up, waiting for the blow. When it came, he took it, grinding his teeth even as he threw a punch.

A deep, powerful voice let out a howl, and was gone.

Brian rested against one of the shelves, taking long, deep breaths, trying to get his heart to calm down. He clutched the iron in his hand.

## Chapter 30: The Battle in the Parlor

Sam and Jenny both looked up to the doorway at the sound of a door being slammed.

Before either of them could say anything the basement door exploded outward and wind came racing into the parlor. The wind was harsh, and cold, and fetid. Sam turned his face away from it, closing his eyes, waiting for the foul wind to pass.

When Sam turned back towards the parlor door, opening his eyes, he saw the thin line of salt had been scattered across the floor. Before Sam could say anything, before Jenny could finish rising to her feet, something came into the parlor.

The room darkened as if a pall was drawn across their eyes, and a horrific chill settled over the room.

"This is our house," a soft, feminine voice said. "How dare you come into it? How dare you seek to drive us out?"

"Your mother raised you better than this, Samuel Hall," another woman said. "She would roll in her grave if she could see you being so disrespectful."

*Paul's mother*, Sam thought. *Dear God help me, I know her voice, she's here.*

The door to the parlor was thrown closed, rattling in the frame as the key was drawn from the lock and vanished from sight.

"Wicked child," Paul's mother whispered, "trapped in a man's body."

"Do you remember your nightmares?" the first voice asked. "I'm sure you do. And you, harlot, why have you shorn your locks? What caused you to cut your hair so short? Have you done something worthy of shame?"

"What the hell?" Jenny asked.

Something metallic squealed from behind them, and Sam turned around. Smoke started drifting out of the fireplace.

One of the dead had closed the flue.

"Shall you join us?" Paul's mother asked. "Shall you, wicked child and shorn harlot, hmm?"

"Perhaps you'll be better folk once you're dead," the first voice chuckled.

"Mm, perhaps," Paul's mother said, "although it did nothing for my boy Paul."

"This is insane," Jenny said softly.

Sam agreed, but didn't speak. He needed to open the flue if the dead would let him.

He walked towards the fireplace and felt something cold, bitterly cold wrap around his right wrist.

*Chosin*, Sam thought. *I was colder than this in Korea.*

Ignoring the cold he pushed on, even as the ghost tried to pull him back.

But he reached the fireplace, and with his left hand opened the flue.

Someone snarled in his ear and pushed him back. Behind him, Sam heard Jenny yelp and a glance showed she was being pulled round the room by her hair.

Out of the corner of his eye, Sam caught sight of a piece of kindling being swung at him. He managed to get out of the way of the wood, saw the fireplace poker in a stand to the right of the hearth and realized that the poker was made of iron.

*Good, wrought iron.*

Sam stumbled, and grabbed a hold of it, his fingers closing around the cold metal. He swung the tool down at the cold grasping his wrist, and someone screamed as the iron made contact.

Catching his balance Sam turned to help Jenny and paused at the sight of Paul's grandfather striding into the room.

The man was as big as Sam remembered him, and as stern in his manner

"Eleanor!" Paul's grandfather called, and suddenly a ghost materialized beside Jenny. It was Paul's mother, her hand wrapped in Jenny's hair, twisting and pulling the young woman's head back, forcing Jenny to her knees.

Eleanor looked at Paul's grandfather, a snarl frozen on her face, her eyes widening.

"Paul won't want you to stop me," she spat. "You know he wants this done."

"Strike, Samuel," Paul's grandfather commanded, grasping hold of his dead daughter-in-law.

And Sam did, the iron passing easily through Eleanor and then through Paul's grandfather as well.

Both ghosts disappeared, and Jenny fell forward, catching herself, gasping for air.

"Brian," she managed to say as Sam helped her to stand. "Brian."

Sam could only nod, gripping the poker tightly and following her out of the room towards the kitchen.

## Chapter 31: Leo and Paul

Leo walked a few steps behind the dead boy, and wondered how long Paul would keep up the charade. *Not too much longer,* Leo believed.

Paul was clever, but he wasn't patient.

The boy wanted to create awe, to create fear. He wanted Leo to believe that there was someone even worse than Paul.

That wasn't so. Not here.

Leo could hear it from the others they passed.

A young man and a young woman whom Paul had drowned in the eighties while they were canoeing.

A middle-aged man who Paul had helped to commit suicide.

And others.

Too many others.

It would take days for all of them to be cleared out. Leo didn't have days. Leo could measure his time in minutes.

*Minutes.* He smiled at the thought, although he knew that when the time came, it would be nothing to smile about.

"You're quiet," Paul said.

"Yes."

Paul laughed, walking on towards a large barn.

The snow continued to fall.

A pair of dead men stood outside of the barn, watching them as Leo followed Paul into the barn.

The interior was dark, nearly black except for the rapidly shrinking rectangle of pale light coming in through the open barn door. Immediately beyond the edge of the light, Paul stopped, and Leo came to a stop, waiting patiently.

"Won't you come in a little farther?" Paul asked.

"Said the spider to the fly," Leo recited.

Paul laughed happily. "Yes. Yes. And I'm the spider."

"We're both flies." Leo said, looking around at the darkness. "Do you know that, Paul?"

Paul paused before answering. "I don't know what you mean."

"No," Leo said. "I don't suppose that you do. But you will soon enough, Paul. You will soon enough."

# Moving In

"I don't like you," Paul said after a minute, and Leo could hear the anger and rage simmering in the dead boy's voice.

"Good."

Paul laughed. "I'm not going to let you go when I kill you. You're going to stay here with me for a very, very long time."

Leo hesitated for a moment before answering. "You're not going to kill me. That's up to the spider. We're just waiting in the web."

"My web!"

"Yes."

"I'm the spider!"

"No," Leo smiled. "You're a fly, Paul. Just a fly."

"I'm going to kill you soon," Paul said, spitting out the words.

Leo sighed. "No. No, you're not. Let's wait together for the spider, shall we?"

Paul laughed. "Alright, Leo. Alright. How long should we wait?"

"One minute past midnight should be enough," Leo said softly.

"Alright, Leo," Paul said cheerfully. "One minute past midnight."

Leo sat down on the dirt floor of the barn and waited for the alarm clock in his head to go off.

# Moving In

## Chapter 32: Back in the Pantry

Brian managed to get himself into a sitting position. Leaning against the shelves, the erratic beating of his heart attempting to unleash panic in his mind, Brian took his heart pills out of his pocket and dry swallowed another one. How the plastic bottle had managed to survive the beating was nothing short of a miracle as far as Brian was concerned.

In the darkness, sitting and waiting for the pill to take effect, Brian wondered suddenly whether or not the sudden attack had been focused solely on him.

Was Leo under attack? Did something try and get in the parlor and attack Jenny or Sam?

Brian needed to know, but he also needed his heart to function normally before he tried to get out of the pantry. Getting out should be simple -- turn the knob on the door.

But Brian had a feeling that it wasn't going to be simple. More than likely it wasn't going to be easy at all.

Brian took long slow breaths, ignoring the shooting pain that came from his ribs with each and every one. His head throbbed, and he knew that as soon as he got out of the pantry he was going to have to get to the bathroom and clean his cuts.

Brian wanted to get out of the house, and he wanted to get out as soon as possible. But he wasn't sure if anyone was going to let him do that either. He also wasn't going leave without Leo.

They were all going to be leaving together.

Taking a deep, steadying breath, Brian got to his feet. He took a small step towards the door, his hand outstretched, fingers seeking the wood.

They met something cold, and Brian stopped.

It wasn't wood.

Flesh.

He could feel flesh beneath his fingers.

Suddenly he could hear breathing, and faintly, right beneath the breathing, Brian could hear the clock in the parlor striking midnight.

"Where is he?" a woman asked.

Brian started to shake. Fear ripped through him at the sound of the woman's voice. She was dead. Brian knew she was dead.

"I...I... who, which he?" Brian said, the words stumbling out of his quivering mouth.

"Leo."

"He went with the boy," Brian whispered. "He went with Paul."

And the flesh disappeared from beneath Brian's outstretched fingers.

With a moan, Brian dropped to his knees again and rested his head against the door. Fear pulled at his guts and magnified the sound of his weak heart beating in his ears.

Moving In

## Chapter 33: Finding Brian

Sam followed Jenny into the hallway, each of them moving carefully. Noise filled the house. Too much noise.

Someone walked from room to room on the second floor. Someone else was screaming in the basement. Terrible screams, curses, and vulgarities that burned even Sam's old Marine Corps ears. The dead sounded enraged, as if something had angered them.

*Was it Leo?* Sam wondered. *Has he done this to them?*

Far above them, in the attic, it sounded as though someone was in the process of destroying an entire, ten service set of china.

*Perhaps they are,* Sam thought. *Perhaps they are.*

Jenny paused by the basement door, closed it and looked back at Sam. "Are you okay?"

Sam smiled at her.

Yes, he liked this young woman. She had more spirit than most people he had ever met.

"I'm fine, thank you," Sam answered. "The kitchen?"

Jenny nodded and led the way once more.

Sam continued to follow her, shifting the poker from one hand to the other. As they advanced down the hall towards the kitchen, the sounds in the house decreased until absolute silence reigned when Jenny paused at the entryway to the kitchen.

"Babe?" she asked softly.

Silence.

"Brian."

Nothing still.

"Brian," Jenny said a little louder into the curious darkness of the room.

"The pantry," Brian answered, his voice muffled.

"I can't see a damned thing," Jenny said.

"Hold on," Sam said. He dug his hand into his jacket pocket, pulled out his flashlight and said, "Watch your eyes. I'm turning on the flashlight."

"Okay," Jenny said, and Sam closed his own eyes as he thumbed the flashlight on. A moment later he opened his eyes as Jenny gasped.

"Damn," Sam murmured.

Before them the kitchen was in shambles. Crockery and dining ware lay scattered about the counters and the floor. The table had been shattered, as were the chairs. The doors of the cabinets had been ripped from their hinges and all of the wood, every stick of it, was neatly set against the pantry door. It looked as though each piece had been nailed in place to keep the door closed, and Sam feared that it had been.

"How," Jenny whispered, stepping into the room, "how is this even possible?"

"How is anything possible?" Sam asked tiredly. "How are the dead here among us? I think that our questions are valid, young lady, and perhaps we can examine them at a later date, but right now I'm fairly certain your husband would enjoy being free of the pantry."

"Very, very true," Jenny said.

She walked into the kitchen and made her way directly to the pantry. Sam watched as she reached up, grabbed hold of one of the cabinet doors and pulled on it. For a moment, the door clung to the rest of the wood before coming away with a tearing sound, as though Jenny had ripped a giant sheet of paper free. She dropped the wood to the floor, where it landed with a harsh, clattering sound in the awkward stillness of the house, and she reached up for the next piece.

Sam shined the flashlight on her work. Nothing, he noticed, was holding the wood in place. No nails, no screws. Something's will alone kept the wood in place, and Sam could only wonder why.

Paul was clever, but never this clever.

This was something else entirely.

## Chapter 34: Said the Spider to the Fly

"Do you want to play?" Paul asked.

Leo looked into the darkness at where he supposed Paul stood.

"What do you want to play?" Leo asked.

*My voice is surprisingly steady,* Leo thought, *considering what's about to happen.*

The seconds were counting down now. The alarm clock's hands moving to their curious and fatal union at the Roman numeral twelve.

"Soldiers," Paul answered.

"What battle?"

The alarm clock chimed cheerfully in Leo's head. It was the same, familiar chime that had greeted him at six o'clock every morning his grandmother had lived with them. Leo smiled. He loved the sound of it, even as he knew what the sound meant.

"Why are you smiling?" Paul asked suddenly. "I don't like the way you're smiling. I want you to stop."

Leo felt strangely relieved. He had feared the alarm clock for so many years. Feared what it meant. And now there was nothing to do about it.

Absolutely nothing.

"Why are you smiling?!" Paul screamed, stepping into the dim rectangle of light cast by the open barn door.

"Why am I smiling?"

"Yes!" Paul howled. The barn around them shook, and Leo's smile widened.

Paul was powerful, extremely so. But not nearly as powerful as he thought.

"Stop smiling!" Paul yelled, taking another step forward. "You stop smiling right now, Leo. You're not nice."

"He has to smile," a soft, female voice said from behind Leo.

Paul's attention snapped onto the voice, and Leo watched him. The boy glared at the speaker.

"Who are you?" Paul demanded. "I don't know you. I didn't kill you. I didn't bind you to me."

"No," the voice said. "But Leo bound me to him, didn't you, Leo?"

Leo could only nod.

"So?" Paul said. "So? What does that have to do with me?"

"Leo's mine, little one," the woman said. "All mine. You go about your business, and all will be well."

"What?" Paul said, angry and surprised. "What?"

"Go away."

Leo watched as rage filled Paul's face.

"Go away?" Paul asked, shaking his head. "This is my land. These are my houses. My dead are around us, and Leo is going to be joining them."

"Go away," the woman said again, her voice lower and the tone softer.

Leo shuddered at the tone.

"You go away," Paul said. "You go away and let me kill him and bind him."

The woman didn't answer, as Leo knew she wouldn't.

A heartbeat later she passed by him on the right, a stunningly beautiful woman wearing an evening gown of dark blue. She moved gracefully, a soft, knowing smile playing across her face. Paul took a cautious step back as she neared him.

"You're nothing," the woman said. "Not even a dream anymore."

Paul looked confused but before he could ask her anything, light exploded out of the young woman and enveloped Paul.

Screams tore through the night and Leo knew that they were from Paul. The ground shook, the wood of the barn creaked. A brutal cold rippled out from the struggle taking place in the barn. Leo's teeth started to chatter and he shook uncontrollably. As the cold passed through him and the barn and reached the trees, Leo heard trees explode.

More screams, torn from the throats of the dead outside of the barn, reached Leo's ears and he winced. He could feel his grandmother's power pulsing, a vicious, malignant heart destroying the ghosts around her.

"Leave!" Paul screamed, his young voice suddenly growing faint. "Leave! This is my place! Mine!"

Leo's grandmother chuckled and the cold spiked out once more.

Paul let out one more abbreviated, outraged howl, and went silent.

The light vanished and Leo's grandmother stood alone. Paul was no more.

Soon enough no one would even remember a boy named Paul had ever existed or lived there on the farm.

The woman turned, smiling at Leo.

"Hello Leo," she said, taking a few steps towards him. "You missed our appointment."

"Yes, grandmother," Leo said softly. "I did."

## Chapter 35: Helpless in the Pantry

Brian found that he could do nothing to help himself out of the pantry. Which was a good thing considering the way his heart continued to keep a completely unnatural rhythm in his chest.

While Jenny worked on the door from the other side, Brian listened to a soft sound; almost a hum. It wasn't electrical, rather it was as though someone was hiding in the farthest reach of the pantry, tucked beneath a shelf, directly above where the bodies were buried in the basement.

Brian closed his eyes and attempted to focus on the sound of Jenny moving things.

Instead, he found himself concentrating on the humming, discovering that he recognized the tune.

It was a hymn. An old hymn that his grandfather had used to sing to him. Brian didn't know the name, but he could hear part of the refrain.

*Give me that old time religion, give me that old time religion, give me that old-time religion, it's good enough for me.*

*Jesus,* Brian thought. *Please, can't this all just be over now? I just want it to be done. I just want it all to be done.*

"Hello, Brian," a young voice said.

Brian didn't answer.

The young voice, belonging to a young woman, let out a giggle.

"You don't want to answer. You're afraid."

Brian forced himself to breathe deeply through his nose. He brought up a memory of Jenny sitting in bed and reading and concentrated on it. He pictured the curve of her shoulder beneath her shirt, the smell of her hair --

"Brian," the voice whispered in his ear. "You can answer me, Brian. I'm not going to hurt you. Some of my friends want to, but not me."

Brian let out a shuddering breath.

"So afraid," the voice said, speaking in his left ear. Something moved gently down his cheek. "So afraid. You don't need to be, Brian. There's nothing really to fear about death.

Especially not here. You never leave so there's no worry about that. Isn't that nice? You can stay with us. You can stay with me. I think you're handsome. Lots of us think you're handsome. Don't you want to stay with us?"

"I don't want to be dead yet," Brian whispered.

The voice let out a gentle laugh. "We all become dead at some point, Brian. I can wait."

Brian kept his eyes closed, listening to Jenny work.

"Yes," the voice said, tracing the line of his chin. "I can wait. But not everyone can. Oh no, Brian. There are others who don't want to wait at all."

From beyond the barred pantry door, someone yelled. Brian realized it was Sam.

# Moving In

## Chapter 36: Sam and Jenny are not Alone

Sam stood close to Jenny as she worked.

The iron poker remained firmly in his hand, and Sam stood in the darkness with the flashlight on the pantry door. From beyond the door, Sam could hear the murmuring of voices and Sam knew from the frenzied way Jenny worked that whatever was being said didn't bode well for Brian.

Suddenly the temperature in the kitchen plummeted.

Sam's breath billowed out, as did Jenny's and the young woman paused.

"This isn't good."

"No," Sam said, nodding in agreement. "This isn't good at all."

The back door blew in violently, bouncing off the wall as the top and middle hinge were torn free of the door frame. A cold, terrible wind raced into the kitchen, ripping the curtains off of the window above the sink and scattering shards of glass and china. Sam's teeth started to chatter, and he took a cautious step to the left, placing himself between the door and Jenny.

"Keep working," Sam said in a low voice.

Jenny's answer was the sound of another piece of wood being torn free.

Sam focused on the open door and brutally cold wind coming in. Snowflakes carried along with the wind, melted as they struck the kitchen floor and the counter top.

Something came in with the snow and the wind.

Something not quite right. Something terrible.

"Stay where you are," Sam said, and his voice was strong, young. A voice called up from his own past.

Whatever it was came to a stop just inside of the kitchen.

"Get out," Sam said. "You are not welcome here."

"Who are you?" a deep, harsh voice demanded. "How dare you attempt to cast me out of my home?"

"This isn't your home," Sam said.

The voice laughed. "Nor is it yours, you foul thing. Come, young one, come and enjoy what little time you have left while we battle one another."

Sam chuckled. All of the fear which had been nestled deep within slipped away.

What did he have to fear? Sam was an old man, and he loved his life. Life was beautiful, powerful, each breath sweet.

Sam had known life's power since he'd come home from Korea.

And he had survived Korea.

To die on the Kenyon farm, well, that would be no hardship, especially while trying to help someone else. Jenny and her husband were fine people, from what he could tell. Maybe, just maybe, Paul and his grandfather might be freed by Leo, too.

"Here," Sam said, handing the flashlight over to Jenny. "Take this. You'll need it."

Without a word Jenny took the flashlight from him and Sam gave the poker a swing.

"Iron," the ghost said.

"Ayuh," Sam replied. "Iron."

"Good," the ghost said, chuckling, and something hurtled through the air, striking Sam in the left thigh.

Sam grunted, stumbled, and caught himself on the back wall.

"Unlike many of my brethren," the ghost said, "I can throw things. Lots of things."

Sam jerked his head to the left, something cut his right cheek, the blood racing down to drip onto his shirt.

"And I love to throw things," the ghost said, laughing happily.

A third object came at Sam in the darkness, and he swung the poker. The two things connected and something shattered.

The ghost spat. "Luck!"

A bowl came racing at Sam, and he struck it down. A tumbler, a shard of a plate.

Sam struck them all.

A small smile crept onto his face.

All those baseball games decades earlier as a kid, hitting a ball he could barely see, one he could hardly hear.

Sam struck down one more, but the one after struck him square in the forehead, sending him to his knees. Dropping the poker, he fell forward. He felt his sternum crack and the air rushed out of him in one long, painful gasp.

*I'm going to die,* Sam realized.

*I'm going to die.*

"Sam!" Jenny yelled, dropping a piece of wood and kneeling down beside him.

Sam couldn't see her. Jenny's voice grew faint.

"The pantry door," Sam said, although he couldn't hear himself. "Open the pantry door."

## Chapter 37: Grandmotherly Love

When Leo had first bound his grandmother to her alarm clock, he had proudly told himself that he would never run when she inevitably slipped free of her binding. He knew, of course, someday he would not make it home in time to reinforce the binding. Just as he knew carrying her, confined to the alarm clock, would be even worse.

*Things get lost.*

*Things get stolen.*

Leo's grandmother would have wreaked havoc on whoever had possession of the clock at the time rather than focusing on Leo, which was what was necessary.

Leo knew, too, roughly how old he would be when his dear grandmother would get free. He knew he would be stronger.

Leo had forgotten, however, about fear.

He had remembered his love for his grandmother, the long nights she had sat up with him and the warmth of her embrace when she was so cold to so many others. Leo had been her first grandchild, beloved above all others.

So he had remembered his love for her and not the fear that settled in as a child when he saw the fates of those who angered her. The devastation which she had wrought even from beyond the grave.

Now, however, as she turned to face him, her cold smile spreading across her face, all of the old fears returned.

Each terrifying fear, each horrific memory.

Leo scrambled to his feet, and he ran.

He ran for the house.

In the curious light of the snow storm, he saw the dead converging on the house.

Something was going on, they all knew it.

Leo knew it too.

The dead were feeding off of the energy of his grandmother. They were growing stronger, the angers and hatreds of their lives manifesting themselves.

And the focus was on the house.

*Brian and Jenny. The man Samuel.*

No, there was Samuel, wandering outside of the house. The man looked confused, seeming to know he was dead but not understanding it.

*I have no time,* Leo thought.

Behind him, he heard the steady steps of his grandmother, the hem of her dress seeming to scrape the snow.

Impossibilities, Leo knew. Tricks.

He heard them all the same, though, and knew she was toying with him.

*She will drag this out,* Leo thought. *She will drag it out as long as she can. Can I blame her? Twenty-five years trapped within the travel clock, the ticking of the gears to keep the mind of such a one occupied.*

No. His grandmother had been too strong for death.

Leo aimed for the back of the house, the direction Sam had come from. Leo doubted that the others had become separated, and since he saw neither Brian nor Jenny he could only hope to find them there.

Leo stumbled once in the snow, caught his footing and managed to stay upright.

The back door was open.

*No,* Leo realized. The back door was blown in and hanging on one hinge.

He leaped up the stairs and into the kitchen to find a man standing amongst the wreckage. Jenny had her back to the ghost as she pulled desperately at the dining table which was jammed against the pantry door.

The ghost, Leo saw, was unbuckling his pants.

The depredations and vile passions of some never left, even after death.

Leo paused a moment, scooped up the iron poker, stepped over the cooling body of Samuel Hall, and lashed out at the ghost.

The iron ripped through the dead man's face, scattering it into the night as it screamed in impotent rage.

Still holding onto the poker, Leo hurried to Jenny's side, helped her tear the table away and push it to the floor as she opened the pantry door. A quick glance in showed Brian's painfully white face and a small woman standing next to him.

With one swift motion, Leo pushed Jenny into the pantry, thrust the poker into the face of the woman and closed the door, plunging them all into darkness.

In the incredibly cramped confines of the pantry, Brain fell backward, and Jenny demanded, "What the hell?!"

"Quiet," Leo said. From a pocket, he pulled out a small bag, a fine mixture of goober dust, sea salt, and iron filings. With a surprisingly steady hand, he opened the bag and tapped out a fine line of the mix onto the pantry floor in front of the door. He wet his index finger, dipped it into the bag and then he carefully touched the doorknob and all three of the hinges.

Leo cleaned off his finger, put the bag away and set the poker down on the floor. He dug out his phone, hit the flashlight app and shined the light down. Glass and debris covered the floor, so he took off his jacket and sat down on it before turning his phone off.

"So," Jenny said in the darkness, "can I just say again, what the hell?"

"Yes," Leo answered.

After a minute of silence, Jenny sighed and said, "Oh Jesus, Leo. What is going on?"

"We're hiding in the pantry," he answered.

Brian let out a weak laugh. "Okay. Tell me, please, why are we hiding in the pantry?"

"We're hiding from my grandmother," Leo answered.

"Your grandmother?" Brian asked. "Why are we hiding from your grandmother?"

"Because she wants to kill all of us," Leo replied.

## Chapter 38: The History of Leo and His Grandmother

Brian leaned back against Jenny, his heart slowly approaching a semblance of normalcy. The pantry was dark, crowded, and thankfully warm with their body heat. When Jenny had first opened the pantry door a cold blast had followed her and Leo and for a brief moment Brian had caught sight of the back door hanging crazily by a single hinge.

Yet now they were locked in the pantry.

Brian liked the man, as strange as Leo was, but being near him was unsettling.

Now, especially so.

Brian cleared his throat before asking, "Why does she want to kill us, Leo?"

Leo was silent for a moment, finally answering, "She is angry with me. And, since you are here, she is angry with you by default."

"She sounds fantastic," Jenny said sarcastically.

"She is," Leo said.

Jenny groaned, and Brian gave her leg a pat. "Could you tell us exactly why your grandmother wants to kill you, Leo?"

"I bound her spirit to an alarm clock."

"Well," Jenny said, "that would definitely piss me off."

"Why," Brian said with a sigh, "did you have to bind her spirit to an alarm clock?"

"She was angry at being dead," Leo said.

"What was she doing?" Brian asked.

"Hurting people."

"How did you know it was her?" Jenny asked.

"I was at her grave," Leo said. "I brought her lilacs. She loves lilacs. When I was at the grave, though, I saw the mark."

"What mark?" Brian asked.

"The mark of spite."

Jenny groaned, and Brian smiled, shaking his head. "Will you tell us now what the mark of spite is?"

"Yes," Leo said. "The mark of spite can be found upon the graves of people who are angry, spiteful, vengeful. The mark of spite is a bare patch of dirt surrounded by grass. The bare patch will be found directly above the heart of the person buried.

These patches can be found in graveyards, burial grounds, cemeteries, and places where the dead are buried but unmarked. You may even find the mark of spite in crypts and mausoleums. Here you will find staining upon the stones and the metal."

Leo sounded as though he had read from an encyclopedia or dictionary.

*Maybe he did*, Brian thought. *Maybe he memorized it all.*

"Okay," Jenny said, "your grandmother had the mark of spite on her grave. Did you start looking for her?"

"Yes," Leo answered.

"We can't ask yes or no questions, Babe," Brian said gently.

"Yeah," Jenny said with a sigh.

"Leo," Brian said.

"Yes?"

"Will you now please tell me how you found your grandmother?" Brian asked.

"Yes," Leo said. He paused a moment before answering, checking his phone. "In thirty-two minutes, I must call Sylvia. If we are still alive."

"Right," Jenny said. "If we're still alive."

"Exactly," Leo said. His phone went dark, and Leo started to speak again. "When I saw the mark of spite I realized it was my grandmother hurting people she had known. She also was hurting people who were in her old house. My grandmother does not like many people."

"Does she like you?" Jenny asked.

"She loves me," Leo answered. "She is only angry with me for binding her to her alarm clock."

"How did you bind her to her alarm clock, Leo?" Brian asked, trying to keep the curious man focused.

"With a binding spell," Leo answered.

Brian took a deep breath.

*Asperger's,* Brian thought. *Leo must have Asperger's.*

"Leo," Jenny said gently, "will you now explain to us how you bound your grandmother? We don't know what a binding spell is, or how to do it."

"Of course not," Leo said. "Most people do not know how to properly use a binding spell. Or any spell, really. The first thing

I had to do was to find a place where my grandmother was going to be. Once I had that, I needed something to bind to my grandmother. Something that was hers and that she had used often."

"And you picked an alarm clock?" Jenny asked.

"Yes. My mother kept everything else. I stole the alarm clock from her. My mother would only have thrown it away."

"Can we stop her?" Brian asked.

"My mother?" Leo said.

Jenny groaned, and Brian said, "No, Leo. Your grandmother. Can we stop her?"

"No," Leo answered. "Not without the alarm clock."

"Is that why you're going to call Sylvia?" Brian asked.

"Yes."

"She'll be able to get the alarm clock for you?" Jenny asked.

"Yes."

"But not until after one?" Brian asked.

"Yes."

"Why --"

Something slammed into the door, cutting her off.

Again and again, the door shook, then suddenly it stopped.

"She cannot come in," Leo said. "The doorknob will not turn for her. The hinges will not work. She could make the wind blow, and the iron dust will keep the line rooted."

"You're not behaving, Leonidas," a woman said.

Her voice was elegant and powerful. A voice full of strength, one evidently used to being obeyed.

"No," Leo said in agreement. "I am not behaving. I thought that I would meet my death in a much braver fashion. I have discovered that I was wrong, Grandmother."

"Do your friends know they're going to die as well?" she asked gently.

"Yes," Leo said. "I have told them that this is the case."

"And they have not cast you out?"

"Not yet."

Leo's grandmother chuckled pleasantly. "I will wait, Leo. I will wait for all three of you. I can hear your male friend's heart, by the way. He is only one good scare away from standing beside me."

Jenny's arms around Brian's waist tightened.

"The young lady," the grandmother continued, "will be much more difficult, I am sure. But you have purchased her death nonetheless, my grandson."

"I know, Grandmother."

"Well, so long as you know, Leonidas."

Silence filled the pantry.

"Jesus...," Jenny said softly after a minute.

"What about him?" Leo asked genuinely wanting to know.

Brian couldn't stop himself from laughing.

# Moving In

## Chapter 39: Sylvia Gets a Text

At exactly one o'clock in the morning, Sylvia's phone sounded off with the Westminster Chimes.

Westminster Chimes.

Sylvia sat up.

Westminster Chimes meant the call was from Leo. Specifically, it meant the call was from Leo's special phone. The one he brought with him to his work. Sylvia threw her blankets off and grabbed her robe up off of her chair, pulling it on as she hurried to her desk. She took her phone off of the charger and looked at it.

*Please use your key. Behind Moby Dick. Bring Clock. Jenny and Brian. Look for Sam. Find the Pantry. Me. Leo.*

Sylvia saw her hands shaking as she texted back, *Okay.*

Outside a plow rumbled by, flashing yellow lights splashing across the drawn shades.

*That's right,* Sylvia thought. *It's snowing.*

Dropping her cell phone into the robe's pocket, she hurried out of the bedroom and down the hall. She forsook her usual attire and pulled on some old jeans and a sweater before tugging on a pair of battered engineer boots.

The heels of the boots echoed off of the hallway's walls as went back to the kitchen. She got on her winter coat, hat, and began pulling on her gloves while heading to the door, scooping up the car keys as she went.

On the sidesteps, Sylvia paused long enough to lock the door before walking through the several inches of snow to her car. With her free hand, Sylvia swept the snow off of the driver's side window, unlocked the car and got in. The heater was just beginning to warm the interior and thankfully the falling snow was light.

Slipping the key into the ignition, Sylvia lowered and raised all of the windows, ignoring the snow that fell into the car. She ran the wipers front and back several times, put the car into gear and edged out to the end of her driveway. A glance left and then right showed the road was clear, so she pulled out and made her way as quickly as she could towards Leo's place.

# Moving In

Beneath the wheels of the car, rock salt popped and cracked, sand bouncing up and hitting the undercarriage. Every sound and every bump magnified.

Something was wrong.

As she came to a set of lights, the Westminster Chimes went off again.

Sylvia tore off her gloves, dug her phone out of her pants pocket and looked at the text.

*Sooner, in this case, is much better than later. That is what Jenny has told me.*

Sylvia didn't wait for the light to turn green.

# Moving In

## Chapter 40: Awaiting One's Fate

Leo put his phone down on his lap and closed his eyes. He was tired.

This was far later than he was used to staying up.

In the darkness, Leo could hear the sound of Jenny and Brian breathing, the two of them synced up into a curious rhythm. Beyond the pantry door, however, Leo could hear things he knew would disrupt the tenuous calm of his hosts.

The dead were active.

Active and angry.

Among the various voices, Leo could hear that of his grandmother.

She was marshaling her forces, preparing to attempt to discover a way into the pantry.

And Leo knew that there must be.

When Jenny had opened the pantry, there had been a female ghost with Brian. Had she come through the door? Leo didn't remember seeing her in the kitchen. She could have slipped in just before he arrived, but that didn't feel right. It didn't feel right at all.

"Brian," Leo said, opening his eyes and looking into the darkness at where he knew the husband and wife to be.

"Yeah?" Brian asked tiredly.

"The ghost that was here with you, where did she come from? Did she come in through the door?"

"I don't know," Brian said, moving around. "How could I know?"

"Where did you first hear her?" Leo asked. He had to remind himself that Brian wasn't stupid, the man merely didn't know anything about ghosts.

"I first heard her behind me," Brian answered after a minute. "From under one of the shelves."

"Jenny?" Leo asked.

"Yes."

"There is probably a heating grate. Could you check?"

"Dang," Jenny said as she bumped into a shelf. "this room's a lot smaller without a proper light."

Leo listened as she worked her way around.

A moment later she said. "Yes, there's an old iron grate back here."

Leo took his pouch from his jacket's inner pocket before reaching out and finding Brian's leg.

"Jesus!" Brian snapped, his leg bouncing up.

"Take this," Leo said, putting the pouch on Brian's leg.

"Okay," Brian said, his voice shaky. "What do you want me to do with it?"

"Hand it to Jenny."

"I have it," Jenny said shortly.

"Good. Open the bag, wet your right index finger, and insert it into the bag."

"Sounds kinky," Jenny said.

Brian laughed, but Leo only frowned.

"How can you hear a kink?" Leo asked, confused. "I designed the pouch so that the opening would not tangle."

Jenny sighed. "Don't worry about it, Leo. Now, what?"

"Remove your finger from the bag. There should be a significant amount of mixture on your finger. Trace the opening of the grate with your finger. Do not remove your finger from the grate until you have gone around the entire edge of the grate. As you move your finger you must whisper, Va Bare Shachiye."

"What the hell does that mean?" Brian asked.

"Bar the path," Leo answered.

"In what language?" Jenny asked.

"Creole."

"Creole?" Jenny asked him.

"Yes."

Brian laughed. "What type of Creole, Leo. Is it Louisiana Creole or Haitian?"

Leo smiled. "You know the difference."

"Yes," Jenny said, "we honeymooned in New Orleans."

"Oh," Leo said. "Very good. Now, make sure you say those words the entire time. It is the only way the mixture can be bound to the grate."

"Okay," Jenny said.

Leo heard her move around even as Brian asked, "Do you think that they're going to try and get in that way?"

"Yes."

"Why?"

"Because they're talking about it right now," Leo said, closing his eyes. "My grandmother is sending them back into the basement."

"No pressure, sweetheart," Brian said softly.

"Nope," Jenny said grimly, "none at all."

*People are confusing,* Leo thought.

As far as Leo could see there was a lot of pressure.

## Chapter 41: Sylvia's Unexpected Meeting

The drive to Mont Vernon took an hour and ten minutes, and Sylvia's hands hurt from gripping the steering wheel.

When she got to Brian and Jenny's house, she saw the taxi parked across the street, exhaust billowing out of the muffler. The windshield wipers dragged across the glass leaving narrow black streaks. In the driveway, under several inches of snow, stood Brian and Jenny's cars.

The house was dark, all of the lights extinguished.

Sylvia turned her car around and backed in carefully. The snow was soft, but it didn't mean she wouldn't have a hard time getting out if she needed to leave in a hurry. Her father had always taught her to back into a driveway if the weather was bad, and she was driving a front wheel drive car.

*Let the car pull you forward,* he had always told her. *It's easier for everyone.*

And it was.

Sylvia smiled at the memory of her father and then she brought herself back to focus on the task at hand: Getting the clock to Leo.

Turning off the car, Sylvia pocketed the key and stepped out into the cold. She closed the door, looked up and fell backward, catching herself against the cold metal.

Someone was standing in front of her, dressed for the cold in an old army uniform. Upon looking closer, she saw that the someone was a young man. His face was barely visible beneath his helmet and hat as well as the scarf wrapped around his neck and lower jaw. He wore huge mittens and heavy boots, and he looked at her with an angry, tired expression on his face.

"I'm dead," the young man said.

"I can see that," Sylvia said softly.

"I don't want to be dead."

"I'm sorry," Sylvia replied.

"So am I."

"Could you help me?" Sylvia asked nervously after a moment.

"Sure."

"I'm looking for someone named Sam."

The young man grinned at her. "I'm Sam."

Sylvia sighed, relaxing slightly. "Leo told me to find you."

The grin disappeared. "He's in trouble. They're all in trouble."

"Why?"

"Leo's grandmother is here."

Sylvia opened her mouth to ask another question, but she closed it as another shape came walking out of the storm from around the house.

The old man whom she had first spoken with.

The farmer.

Sam turned, saw the man and waved.

The older ghost nodded.

"Have you met Fred?" Sam asked her. "Fred is Paul's grandfather."

"I've met him," Sylvia said softly. "Where is Paul?"

"Gone," Fred answered.

"Was he the one holding you here?"

Fred gave a curt nod.

"So you can leave now?"

"No," Fred said. "Leo's grandmother is keeping us here now."

"Why?" Sylvia asked.

"She wants to kill Leo," Sam answered. "And Brian and Jenny. She's mad at Leo for something."

"Leo said something about a pantry," Sylvia said after a moment. "I have to bring him something."

"She's in the kitchen, with the other ghosts," Sam said.

"It is not a safe place to enter," Fred added. "You will be risking your life if you enter. More importantly, young lady, your soul will remain trapped here as well."

"I figured that," Sylvia said. "But I have to get to Leo."

"Good," Fred said. "I like determination. Follow me, please."

Fred turned around and started to walk through the fresh snow, his steps never disturbing the beauty of the snow covered landscape.

Sylvia followed Fred. Sam, in turn, followed Sylvia.

They made their way around the side of the house, and then to the back of it. Sylvia saw what she assumed was the back door to the kitchen.

The three of them stopped a short distance from the exposed room, and Sylvia could see the various ghosts moving quickly within.

"What are we going to do?" Sylvia asked softly.

"Sam and I are going into the kitchen," Fred replied. "You'll follow. You will go directly to the pantry. The door to it is narrow and tall. Sam and I will hold the others off."

"Okay," Sylvia said, flexing her hands nervously, "let's get this done."

"Agreed," Fred said, and Sylvia watched the two ghosts advance on the kitchen.

# Moving In

## Chapter 42: Leaving the Pantry

Brian started to drift off to sleep, comfortable in Jenny's embrace when he heard Leo gasp. *There is no way this is a good thing.*

"Leo," forcing himself to stay awake, Brian asked. "What's happening out there?"

"I just heard Sam's voice," Leo said. "He's coming into the kitchen."

"Is that good?"

"Yes," Leo said after a moment. "Yes. He's coming in, and he's not alone."

"Who's coming with him?" Jenny asked.

"The grandfather," Leo replied.

A light glowed suddenly, causing Brian to blink. Leo had taken his phone out of his pocket and was looking at it.

"Good," Leo said, and he put the phone away.

"What's good?" Jenny asked.

"Sylvia is here."

"Did she bring the clock?" Brian asked.

"Yes."

Jenny's grip tightened, and Brian gave her a reassuring pat on the hand.

"Leo, is she on her way in?" Brian asked.

"Yes."

"Good," Brian said. "Very good."

Something shattered in the kitchen, and someone let out an angry, rage filled scream.

More and greater sounds of violence followed, the floor starting to shake underneath them. Brian focused on his heart, on keeping it beating steadily.

"She's coming," Leo said softly.

"Who?" Brian asked.

"My grandmother," Leo said. "I fear that she will be going after Sylvia."

There was a scraping sound within the pantry and when Leo spoke again his voice was coming from above them.

"I will be opening the door in a moment," Leo said. "I cannot let my grandmother hurt Sylvia."

"Should we go out with you?" Jenny asked.

"That is your decision," Leo said. "But they will kill you whether you are sitting in the pantry or fighting in the kitchen."

"Well," Jenny said, "I guess I know what I'm doing."

"Me too," Brian said, and together they stood up in the darkness. His body was stiff, and each movement was painful. His ribs screamed with each deep breath he took, and it felt as though the cuts from the broken light bulb had reopened, blood trickling out of the wounds.

*Oh yeah,* Brian thought as he suppressed a groan. *I'm in great shape.*

"Sylvia is coming in," Leo said, and Brian heard the man turn the doorknob, opening them to the attacks of the dead.

## Chapter 43: The Ghastly Spectacle

When Sylvia stepped into the kitchen, she saw more ghosts than she had ever seen in her life.

She had seen the dead occasionally, ever since she was a little girl. Almost all of them had been bemused, or benevolent. Of course, there had been the rare wretched ones, but those had truly been the exceptions.

In the house, though, in the destroyed room before her, Sylvia saw not only the dead but her own death waiting for her as well.

Sam and the grandfather fought against the others, a struggle frighteningly physical. Some of the combatants were nothing more than the faintest of images, others were nearly fully formed. They ranged in age and differed in gender, yet all of them were led by a tall, beautiful woman standing near the hallway.

Leo's grandmother.

Sylvia recognized the woman from the photograph which Leo had once shown her.

She was a striking woman, one who bore the stamp of royalty and intelligence.

And the woman was looking at Sylvia.

The small, travel alarm clock in Sylvia's hand suddenly became cold and heavy.

Sylvia looked around quickly and caught sight of the pantry door. She started to run to it, her boots kicking aside broken dishes and scattered wood. A huge, ethereal arm reached out to grab her, and suddenly Sam was there. The young man managed to push the arm aside and wedge himself between her and the hulking spirit attempting to stop her.

Out of the corner of her eye, Sylvia saw Leo's grandmother advancing towards her.

As Sylvia neared the pantry, she saw the knob turn and the door spring out.

And Leo stepped out into the spiritual battlefield.

His grandmother stopped, smiling at him.

Leo gave her a small smile in turn. He glanced at Sylvia, his smile actually widening with pleasure.

Sylvia held out the alarm clock, and Leo took it.

Even as the smile on Leo's grandmother's face vanished, Brian, supported heavily by Jenny, stumbled out into the kitchen.

Sylvia hurried to them and got on Brian's other side. Together the three of them retreated several steps to stand near the sink.

"I will not go back, Leo," his grandmother said clearly.

"I am not offering you a choice, Grandmother," Leo said. A small tremor-filled his voice and Sylvia heard the hidden terror in her friend's voice.

"I didn't believe that you were," his grandmother said with a smile. She glided forward a few feet.

"You must go back," Leo said. He straightened up slightly. "You should, by all rights, Grandmother, have moved past this place."

She scoffed at him. "Please, Leo. What do you think waits for you after death?"

"I do not think about it."

His grandmother smiled. "And that is why I love you so, dear Leonidas. You do not worry over much, do you?"

"No, Grandmother, I do not."

With a flick of his wrist, Leo opened the alarm clock.

His grandmother lashed forward faster than Sylvia could see. Blackness exploded out into the room, and voices screamed out in pure terror. Sylvia realized that one of the voices was her own.

## Chapter 44: In the Kitchen

When Brian could finally see, he realized that Leo was on the floor, crumpled on his side. The body of Sam was a few feet away. Jenny stiffened slightly, and Brian said, "I know, Babe. I know."

"The door," Jenny said.

Brian nodded and leaned against the wall as Jenny let go of him. He watched his wife shove the kitchen door back into the frame, forcing the deadbolt into place.

Brian looked over at Sylvia, who had sat down on the floor. She took Leo's head into her lap. His glasses were gone, part of the debris-covered floor, and he looked much younger as he smiled at Sylvia. His hands were curled around a battered and broken antique travel clock.

The man's mouth moved, but Brian couldn't hear anything.

Sylvia leaned closer, her body hiding Leo's face from Brian.

Jenny came over in silence and wrapped her arms around Brian, helping him to stand straight once more.

Brian watched as Sylvia nodded, reached out and slipped a hand into one of Leo's pockets, and took out the small book Leo had been walking around with.

"Yes," Sylvia said softly. "Yes. Yes, I'll do it, Leonidas."

She gently set Leo's head on the floor.

Suddenly a wind sprang up, seeming to explode from Leo's limp form. Small fragments of glass and scattered napkins were dragged into a miniature whirlwind. The house shook and the windows rattled in their frames.

Brian and Jenny staggered backwards while Sylvia remained where she was, her head down. She remained untouched even though she knelt in the center of the storm. Brian watched her nod once as she reached out, brushed a stray lock of hair off of Leo's forehead and then leaned in to give Leo a kiss.

The wind vanished and for a moment the room was filled with the clatter of broken crockery falling to the damaged kitchen floor.

"What did he say...before he died?" Jenny asked in a low voice.

"He wants us to help them; the dead," Sylvia whispered. "All of us."

Brian looked at the strange ghost trapper on the floor. For the briefest of moments fear threatened to overwhelm him, but he fought it down. He had faced more than he ever thought he could, and Leo, evidently, thought he could do so again.

"But why?" Brian asked finally. "Why us? Why me?"

"Because you've been surrounded by ghosts every day for weeks, and you're still sane. When asked, Leo says you fought without question, and more than that, you survived. Leo thinks the pair of you, and me, are some sort of exception to most people."

"He told you that as he died?"

"Kind of. He said a lot without words. It's like a feeling. Someone has to help them. And he saw something in you Brian, a kind of kindred spirit. I don't know what."

"Well that makes two of us," Brian replied, perplexed.

"Well, babe?" Jenny looked at Brian with a wry smile. It was the same smile she had given him on the date she realized she had fallen in love with him. "I'm game if you are."

Brian sighed. It had been a hell of a night.

Jenny gave him a tight hug and Brian realized that the house felt empty.

The dead were gone from the old Kenyon farm, but now he knew there were others, and he felt a sudden sense of purpose come over him.

It was a feeling he thought he would probably live to regret, but what the hell, he was going to do it anyway. After all, he considered, it wouldn't be the first time he'd changed careers.

"OK, Leo. We'll do it."

But first, Brian was going to have a drink.

\* \* \*

## Bonus Scene Chapter 1: Kenyon Farm, August 1973

Paul Licata and David Keene each took a long drink of water from their canteens and sat on a fallen log. They were drenched with sweat from working in the summer heat, their shirts long since abandoned. David's feet seemed to swim in sweat inside his workboots and both of their jeans were covered with pine sap. The two young men were exhausted and they still had to make camp.

Directly in front of them was Paul's VW bus, but they had managed to effectively hide it with pine boughs and tree limbs, as well as splashing mud from the nearby stream on it. A random stranger could pass within ten feet and never know the bus was there. David didn't think that any State police would think to look this far out, but they couldn't risk it.

Paul had messed up.

He'd killed the bartender when they'd robbed the Tavern two nights earlier and now, at eighteen, they were both looking at life in prison. David had made sure to drive down into Massachusetts just to make sure that any New Hampshire people who saw the van saw it going south. They'd spent the next night making their way up back roads to hide in Mont Vernon.

Luckily they had found a farm, out on the end of Old Nashua Road. David had scouted it out for a while, and all he had seen was one old farmer walking in and out of a barn and working on a pickup truck that looked like it had been built before the Japanese had bombed Pearl Harbor.

"When do you want to make camp?" Paul asked. He'd been quiet for a long time.

"Soon," David answered. "Need a breather."

Paul nodded.

After a few minutes, Paul asked, "How long do you want to stay here?"

"Maybe a day, maybe a week" David said. "I want to see if the farmer leaves. Maybe we can grab some food out of his house, even siphon off some gas. We won't be able to stop anywhere for fuel. We'll have to steal it whenever we can."

"Yeah."

"We'll be alright, Paul," David said. "Couple of days we'll be in Canada. From there we can cut across the country towards the west coast. Maybe Vancouver."

Paul sighed. "Let's just get the camp set up for now. If you're ready."

"I am." David stood up and stretched. "Okay, let's get this done."

## Bonus Scene Chapter 2: The Farmer Leaves

The sound of an engine starting woke David up. He lay on his back, eyes open and listened. The rumble of the engine told him that it was old, well-maintained, but old.

The farmer's truck.

David got up and walked out from under the tarp they'd strung up between a trio of trees and left Paul sleeping on the ground. Quietly, David made his way to the edge of the road and dropped down behind a tree.

In the distance he could see the farmer's red pickup turning around in the yard and then driving out onto the road. Within a few moments, it was gone from sight.

Hurrying back to Paul, David woke his friend up.

"Hey."

"What?" Paul asked tiredly.

"The farmer left."

"What farmer?"

"The farmer, dumb ass."

Paul blinked several times and then his eyes widened. "Oh. That farmer."

"Exactly."

"Good," Paul said, getting out from under the tarp. "I'm hungry as hell."

David nodded and rubbed his hand over his stomach. They hadn't eaten since before the robbery.

They moved out of their small campsite and quickly made their way to the house. They slipped around to the back and found the kitchen door unlocked. David went in first, cautious and listening.

The old man's refrigerator made some noise, but other than that the house was silent.

No one else was in it as far as David could tell.

When he stepped further into the kitchen, Paul followed him and together they went searching through the cabinets and then the pantry. David found a dusty, empty rush basket and the two of them started to load it up with canned goods and half a dozen apples out of a barrel by the fridge. They moved quickly, and when they had the basket filled, David looked over at Paul.

"Should we check the rest of the house?" he asked.

Paul nodded.

David picked the basket up and let Paul take the lead.

The house was clean, but sparsely furnished. Old family photographs in oval frames hung on the walls, but the rooms showed their age in worn rag-rugs and faded wallpaper. The upholstery on the few pieces of furniture were threadbare, but the rifles and shotguns they found in a gun cabinet were well cared for and neatly arranged. They each took a shotgun, full-length double-barreled Remingtons. They also found a box of shells loaded with birdshot.

"Good enough?" Paul asked.

"Yes," David said, nodding. "Let's get out of here."

They turned to leave, but the sound of a door opening froze them in place.

David hadn't heard the farmer's truck. The windows around the house were open. They should have heard any vehicle approaching the house in plenty of time to get out. But they hadn't.

The two of them stood still as they listened to the sound of footsteps approaching, moving steadily along the hallway that led back to the kitchen. A heartbeat later the footsteps were just before the open doorway, and then they were passing by.

Yet there was nothing visible.

No one belonged to the footsteps.

The sound continued down the hallway, and then seemed to go up a set of stairs. A few moments later David could hear the person moving on the second floor. David tilted his head up slightly to look at the ceiling. The footsteps ceased only to be followed by the squeak of an old box-spring and the settling of a bed.

"What was that?" Paul whispered.

"A big old clue," David said, swallowing nervously, "that we should get out of the house and back to the Volkswagen."

Paul nodded his agreement, and the two of them hurried out of the house as fast and as quietly as they dared.

Within a few minutes, they were back in the relative safety of their camp, sitting just outside of the tarp, and had relaxed. The shotguns and shells were placed on the ground, and the two of them quickly picked out something to eat.

David used the can opener on his keychain to open a can of baked beans, which he ate greedily, tilting the can up and into his mouth. They were both ravenous. Neither he nor Paul spoke as they ate, pausing in their chewing to drink water from their canteens.

When David finished with the beans, he added a little water to the can, swirled it around and then he drank the water. Belching loudly, he put the can on the ground and looked at Paul, who was finishing an apple, core and all. Paul took a long drink from his canteen, capped it and set it on the ground before looking at David.

"We need to get out of here tonight," David said.

"Yeah," Paul said. "That was a ghost in there, wasn't it?"

"What else could it be?" David asked in return. "I mean, I doubt the guy's got the invisible man living with him."

"Yeah."

"Doesn't matter," David continued. "We've got enough food to last us a day or two. We can start tonight a couple hours after sunset."

"Okay," Paul said, picking up another apple. "Okay."

## Bonus Scene Chapter 3: NightFall

David cleared off the last of the branches from the VW as the sun set and while Paul vomited again behind a fir tree.

The apples had gone right through him, and he had been sick immediately after finishing them. David tried not to listen to the heaving noises Paul was making, or the foul smell that followed, and instead focused on getting the VW ready to travel. He reloaded the little camping gear that they had and stowed away the food.

Paul was still sick.

Shaking his head David walked to the driver's side, got in, and turned the key in the ignition.

Nothing happened.

David tried it again.

Still nothing.

"Shit," David grumbled to himself. He started walking back towards the engine when he smelled it.

Oil.

The odor up close was so strong that even the stench of Paul's regurgitated stomach contents couldn't conceal it.

Groaning, David got down on his hands and knees and looked under the VW. In the last light of the sun that managed to filter through the trees, David saw a large puddle of oil glistening on the leaves beneath the engine.

Paul came out from behind the fir tree as David pushed himself into a sitting position, resting his back against a tire.

"Everything okay?" Paul asked.

David shook his head.

"What's wrong?"

"Oil leak," David said. "Looks like the whole pan's emptied out onto the ground."

"Oh shit," Paul said, sitting down across from David and wincing.

"Yup," David replied.

"Well, how the hell are we supposed to get out of here?" Paul asked. "We can't hang around in New Hampshire. Hell, we can't even hang around in the States."

"I know," said David.

"We can't fix the damn thing."

"Jesus Christ, Paul," David said, "I know that we can't. Let's try and figure out what it is that we can do, okay?"

Paul nodded.

After a moment Paul said, "What about the farmer's truck?"

"Steal it?"

"Yeah," Paul said. "Old truck or not, we're looking at a murder rap. I don't see we have much choice."

David nodded slowly. For some reason, he felt bad about the idea. "We've got to get out of here."

David nodded again, sighing. Stealing some of the old man's food was one thing. Stealing his truck was something else. "Maybe he's got another ride in the barn?"

"You think?"

"I don't know," David said. "I saw him going in and out of the barn a few times today before he took off."

"Okay," Paul said, "we can check it out. But we need to go."

"Soon as it's dark enough we'll go to the barn, and then to the truck if we need to. We can hotwire the damned thing if we need to."

David got to his feet and went to the passenger's side door, reached in and pulled out the two shotguns and the box of shells. He brought everything back to where Paul was and sat down, handing one of the shotguns to Paul. David opened the box of shells and set it between the two of them. Quietly the two of them broke open the weapons and loaded them. Each of them stuffed their pockets with spare rounds.

A soft humming sound drifted out from the woods. Someone was out there with them, humming a tune that seemed vaguely familiar to both of them.

David frowned, listening, trying to identify it.

"That's the battle hymn of the republic," Paul said softly, turning his head to look towards the sound.

David looked as well but couldn't see anything. But there was something wrong, not with the tune, but with what was missing. He couldn't hear the sound of anyone walking. He should have been able to hear the noise of boots crunching through dead leaves and fallen pine needles.

The humming came closer, and louder.

David's heart quickened its beat and nearly leaped out of his mouth. Suddenly Paul groaned, and doubled over in pain, staggering. He dropped his shotgun, clutched his lower stomach and fell onto his side.

The humming grew louder and then, just, stopped.

"Too many apples perhaps?" a voice asked.

David couldn't see anything or anyone. The voice spoke from right in front of him, but he couldn't see the speaker.

"Oh yes," the voice said, chuckling. "Far too many apples. Never a good thing."

Paul whimpered and lost control of his bowels.

"I don't know if fear or the apples are responsible for that," the voice said, laughing cheerfully. "But I'm thinking fear more than anything else, aye, boy?"

David opened his mouth to reply, but the blast of a shotgun interrupted him, the sound deafening him while the blast blinded him briefly. The voice let out an enraged shriek and fell silent.

"Come on," a voice said from behind.

David twisted around and saw the old farmer standing there, reloading a shotgun and putting the spent shells into a pouch on his side.

"Grab your friend and move," the old farmer said, "Henry's not out here alone, and they don't like strangers."

David scrambled to his feet, grabbed hold of Paul and pulled him up.

"Move if you want to live," the old farmer said, and he turned his back on them and began marching back toward the old farm house.

Nearly carrying Paul, David stumbled in his haste to follow the old man, yet David kept to his feet.

He kept moving.

David wanted to live.

Bonus Scene Chapter 4: In the House Again

David left Paul in the small parlor, half-asleep on the settee. David walked into the kitchen and accepted a beer from the old man.

"Next time, ask," the old man said.

David nodded.

The old man gestured to the table and sat down. David followed suit and sat opposite.

"What's going on here?" David asked, uncomfortable.

"Death," the old man said. "A lot of it, when they can get it."

"Who?"

"The dead. Well, some of them. Some like Henry."

"Who the hell is Henry?"

The old man smiled tightly. "Henry was a great-uncle of mine. Died at a place called 'The Sunken Road' during the Civil War. He's a right bastard. Has a taste for killing, if he can manage it."

"How can you live here?" David asked. He took a long drink as the old man's words struck home. "I mean, don't they try and kill you?"

"I'm family," the old man answered.

"How many have they killed?"

"Can't rightly say," the old man said. "I have a lot of property. Occasionally I find animals dead. No reason for it; just dead, and not where they should be. Some of the family members are alright, though. Even pleasant at times."

"How long have you lived with them?" David asked.

"All my life," the old man answered. "I was born here. Left for a little bit to fight in France during the Great War, but that was the only time. Haven't even been down into Nashua since we were fighting in Korea."

"So you grew up with ghosts?"

"Yes," the old man said, matter-of-factly.

"And they don't bother you?"

The old man chuckled. "I didn't say that, young man. Some of them don't bother me. Some of them do. They're relatives, just relatives who happen to be dead. My name's Fred Kenyon, by the way."

"David Keene," David replied. He extended his hand, and the old man shook it. The hand was strong and calloused.

"Running?"

"Yeah."

"From what?"

David paused for a moment, and then he said, "We held up the Tavern in Nashua. Paul got carried away, and killed the bartender. He didn't mean to, just an unlucky punch," he added.

"Never a good thing," Fred said softly.

David shook his head.

"You're running together?"

"Yeah."

"Why?"

"He's the closest thing I have to family," David said. "We grew up together on a tough little street in Nashua. Didn't realize it was a shit hole until we were old enough to take a good look around some of the rest of the city. Anyway, we'd been cutting lawns and doing odd jobs to get some money up for traveling. Thought it would be a good idea to roll the bartender at the Tavern. Turns out it wasn't. Just wanted to see the rest of the country."

"I understand," Fred said, finishing his beer. "I didn't realize how big the world was until I sailed across the Atlantic. Nothing like an ocean to make you realize that you really don't mean all that much to the world."

Fred stood up, put the empty bottle on the counter and went to the fridge. "Want another?"

"Please," David said. He put his empty down on the table. Fred returned a moment later with two opened bottles. "Thanks."

"You're welcome," Fred said.

A creak sounded behind David, and he turned in his seat, and he saw nothing.

"Mary?" Fred asked.

The cabinet above the fridge opened, revealing a bottle of whiskey. David watched, unable to look away as something took the bottle out of the cabinet and over to the counter. Once the bottle was put down the cabinet to the left of the sink opened and a pair of tumblers were taken out. David continued to watch as the bottle was uncorked and the liquor was poured into each of the glasses.

The bottle was capped, returned to the cabinet above the refrigerator, and then the cabinet door was closed.

"Thank you, Mary," Fred said gently, and the sound of someone walking away filled the kitchen for a moment.

"Mind fetching those?" Fred asked.

"Um, sure," David said. He got up, took the tumblers and brought them back. He handed one to Fred before sitting down.

"Mary," Fred said, taking a small sip of the whiskey, "was my great-uncle Henry's second wife. She's a lovely woman. Very quiet, very helpful. I'm suspecting that my great-uncle was rather fond of his drink, though. All she does is ply me with alcohol."

"She just wants to get drinks for you?" David asked.

"Yes," Fred said. "And when I was a little boy after my mother had passed away, Mary used to sing to me."

"Your mother?" David started.

Fred shook his head. "No. My mother is not among the ghosts here. When I was a little boy, I used to wish that she was. I missed her terribly, of course, but as an adult I realized it was better for her to have moved on."

"Who else is here?" David asked.

"Others," Fred said. "Others."

David watched as the man finished his whiskey in one long gulp.

"You should check on your friend," Fred said. "Want some eggs?"

"Please," David said. He left both of his drinks on the table and went into the parlor.

Paul wasn't on the settee.

Paul wasn't in the room at all.

"Fred," David called.

A moment later Fred was in the doorway.

"Son of a bitch," the old man grumbled. "Where the hell did they take him?"

"What do you mean?" David asked, turning around to face the old man. "How the hell can a ghost take someone?"

"They just can," Fred snapped. "Don't worry about the why, boy, we need to find him. Damn me for not checking on him."

David followed Fred out of the room and into the hallway. They traveled up a long flight of stairs.

"Check these rooms," Fred said, motioning towards the five doors on the second floor. "I'll check the attic."

"Okay," David said. He walked quickly to the farthest door and opened it.

David found himself looking in on a room that hadn't been touched in years, if not decades. The dust was thick on the furniture, a sheet hung over what had to be a mirror. The shades were drawn, and the room was silent.

Terribly silent.

A slight motion caught his eye and David turned his head to the left to look at a tall, cane-backed rocker. No dust had been allowed to settle on the chair, and it rocked ever so slightly as David looked at it.

Beside the chair was a closed door. More than likely a closet.

*He can't be in there. He can't,* David thought. *But I have to check. It's Paul. Oh, Jesus Christ, I have to check.*

Taking a deep breath, which failed miserably at calming his nerves, David stepped into the room. The chair stopped rocking, and David could feel someone watching him. Someone listening to every sound that he made. Someone feeling the heat of his body.

David's mouth dried out as he crossed the floor, the squeak of each board sounding like the scream of someone being murdered.

*Don't think about murder,* David thought.

He reached out and took hold of the brass doorknob to the closet door and turned it.

Someone turned it back the other way from the inside.

David wet himself just a little, but he turned the doorknob again. Nothing resisted. Sweet Jesus, David thought, let this damned thing be empty.

Pulling the door open David braced himself for whatever was in the closet.

Not a thing.

Nothing except dust and ancient mouse droppings along the back wall.

David closed the closet door and stepped back, breathing quickly.

The rocker started to move again in a slow, steady rhythm. The closet's doorknob rattled, and David backed nervously out of the room. He closed the door behind him and paused in the hallway to catch his breath. He still had four doors to open. Four rooms to look into.

Four more opportunities to be scared to death.

David walked to the next door, found it unlocked, and went into the room. Unlike the first, this room was clean and well-kept. There were pictures of what were probably Fred's family on his dresser, pictures in old silver frames. The narrow twin bed was made, shoes neatly placed beside the closet.

Taking a deep breath David walked to the closet and opened it.

Flannel shirts were hung on hangers, old jeans folded neatly on a shelf beside a gray fedora. A pair of winter boots and several wooden boxes labeled, "Photos," stood beside them.

Sighing with relief David closed the door and heard a thump.

He turned and looked around the room.

The thump sounded again, from beneath the bed. David would have to get down on his hands and knees to look. A plain blue bed skirt hid what was under the bed.

David got down, leaned only as close as he had to in order to lift up the skirt, and looked in at the semi-darkness beneath the bed.

All David saw were the floorboards and the barest hint of dust. He --

"Shh," a young voice said directly in front of him, "don't tell Frederick that I'm here."

David scrambled backward, falling over himself and unable to calm down until his back struck the frame of the door painfully.

"Don't tell him," the voice said from under the bed. "We're playing hide and seek, and he's it. He doesn't know it, but he is."

The dead child laughed, the sound filling the room.

David got to his feet, fled the room and slammed the door closed behind him.

Three more doors. *Jesus Christ, I don't think that I can do three more doors.*

But he had to find Paul.

Above him David heard talking, and he looked up, listening.

"Where the hell did you put him?" David heard Fred ask.

A pause followed the question.

"Yes, I want to know. Helen, Helen just tell me where you put the boy."

Silence.

"I don't want to play any games, Helen," Fred said, "I just want to find the boy."

David held his breath and then let it out slowly.

"You know what the others will do," Fred snapped. "Just tell me where he is Helen. Helen, oh Jesus Helen don't pout. You can't just take someone."

Something moved in the attic.

"I don't care if Jonathan is playing hide and seek," Fred said, "I'm not. And that boy Paul isn't playing either."

Footsteps sounded as someone walked away from David's side of the house.

"Oh damn it, Helen," Fred said.

David listened to the footsteps fade away, and a moment later a heavier pair rang out. Soon Fred was descending the stairs from the attic, a frown on his face. "How many rooms do you have left?"

David held up three fingers.

"Are you okay?" Fred asked.

David shook his head.

"Buck up, son," Fred said. "Let's find your friend."

Fred turned and entered the room closest to him, and David looked at the next door, hesitating just for a minute. The ghosts hadn't hurt him, only frightened him. Maybe the ones in the house were okay. Maybe.

Opening the door, David stepped into the room and felt himself being picked up and thrown, slamming into the floor, the wind rushing out of him. His chest throbbed with pain, and there was a sharp, burning sensation in his right lung. David rolled onto his back, trying to breathe.

Gasping, he straightened up, stopped and then he let out a scream.

The room he was in was barren of any furniture. No sign of life, especially not from Paul who hung from the ceiling, his ankles tied and the rope looped over an iron hook set into the ceiling's cracked plaster. Paul's fingertips brushed the worn wood floorboards and the look of horror on his face was terrifying to see.

"Henry," Fred snarled from the doorway. "David, get out of the room."

David started, slowly, and then Fred stepped in, grabbed David by the collar of his shirt and dragged him out into the hall. Fred slammed the door shut.

"You need to get downstairs, into the kitchen," Fred said. "Stay there. Don't move until I come back and get you."

"Where are you going?" David asked, standing up uneasily.

"I have to deal with Henry," Fred said. "And I have to try and get your friend's body back."

"What do you mean try?"

"Henry likes to keep his trophies. He loves the hunt. Don't know why he thought your friend would be a prize since there was no chase," Fred said, shaking his head. "Evidently he does, though."

David couldn't move for a moment, stunned by what he had seen.

"Downstairs, David," Fred said. "Downstairs. Go to the kitchen."

Without a word David went down the stairs to the first floor. He stayed focused on getting to the kitchen, but he could feel eyes upon him. People watching. People who should be dead. Lots of them. Too many of them.

When he reached the kitchen, David turned on the light and went to the table. Standing beside it David finished his whiskey and his beer.

*What am I doing here?* David thought. *I need to leave. I can't stay in the kitchen. What if Henry comes in? How is Fred going to stop him?*

David realized that he was shaking, and he grabbed hold of the back of the chair to steady himself.

"I need to go," David said. "I need to go."

Letting go of the chair he walked stiffly to the back door, opened it and looked out into the night sky. Beyond the glow of the kitchen, which cast light out onto the ground, the land was dark. The stars shined through the haze of the August night, but there were no street lights. No light slipping out of shop windows to show the way.

*I need to go.*

David left the kitchen, walking down the steps and started across the grass. He aimed at the rows of young corn growing in the distance and slowly quickened his pace.

Soon he was running towards them, and then he was in the corn. He was taller than the stalks, so he could see everything. Just on the opposite side of the cornfield, David saw the forest, the tree line wrapping around the acres of corn. If he could get through the corn he could circle around to the highway, the highway was to the North. He could hitch a ride, see how far he could get.

A crash sounded, and David jerked his head to the right.

Something huge was rushing from the far edge towards him. The corn was being smashed aside and crushed under something's foot.

David couldn't see it.

There was no denying that the thing was still coming, though and that it was aiming for David, but David couldn't see it. He couldn't see it at all.

David tried to run faster, but the thing chasing him increased its own speed.

From behind him David heard the crash of a shotgun, first one round, and then a second.

Still the thing kept running. Still kept getting closer.

David tried to turn, slipped, stumbled, got to his feet, and found himself hurtled backward. The pain in his chest, which had briefly been drowned out by the thrill of escaping returned, bringing tears to his eyes. David found that he couldn't move. Nothing responded to him except for his eyes. Those he could move and all that he saw was corn and the sky

David could hear, though. He could hear whatever it was stepping closer to him, seeming to snort. David breathed with difficulty, trying to ignore a foul scent that seemed to have accompanied the thing which had struck him down.

From the right came the sound of the shotgun again, and this time the thing stopped.

"Get away from him, you dumb son of a bitch," Fred said tiredly, stepping into David's circle of vision. The old farmer was calmly breaking down the shotgun and reloading. "Get on and get."

A long pause followed, and then the thing grunted and walked off, the corn parting around it as it left.

Fred walked over to Henry and squatted down slowly, groaning a little.

"Are you alright?" Fred asked.

David couldn't answer. He couldn't do anything other than look and listen.

Fred frowned. "More'n likely he broke your back. You won't make the ride to the hospital. I suspect that you wouldn't want to, neither. Aside from possibly losing permanent control of everything and then being brought to prison that way. No, that wouldn't be good."

David looked at Fred.

"I wish that you hadn't run," Fred said, giving David a sad smile. "I was dealing with Henry. Everything would have worked out; except for what happened to Paul, of course. I could have gotten you away. You just had to stay in the kitchen."

David felt tears well up in his eyes, and he was ashamed. He didn't want to cry. Men were never supposed to cry.

"There's only one thing we can do now," Fred said, standing up. "I'm sorry that this happened, David. Truly I am. If you don't move on, you're welcome to visit."

Fred smiled at David, brought the shotgun up to his shoulder and sighted along the barrel.

David closed his eyes as Fred squeezed the trigger.

\* \* \*

## FREE Bonus Novel!

Wow, I hope you enjoyed this book as much as I did writing it! If you enjoyed the book, please leave a review. Your reviews inspire me to continue writing about the world of spooky and untold horrors!

To really show you my appreciation for purchasing this book, please enjoy a **FREE extra spooky bonus novel.** This will surely leave you running scared!

Visit below to download your bonus novel and to learn about my upcoming releases, future discounts and giveaways: www.ScareStreet.com

### FREE books (30 – 60 pages):
### Ron Ripley (Ghost Stories)
1. Ghost Stories (Short Story Collection)
   www.scarestreet.com/ghost

### A.I. Nasser (Supernatural Suspense)
2. Polly's Haven (Short Story)
   www.scarestreet.com/pollys
3. This is Gonna Hurt (Short Story)
   www.scarestreet.com/thisisgonna

### Multi-Author Scare Street Collaboration
4. Horror Stories: A Short Story Collection
   www.scarestreet.com/horror
5. Terror in the Shadows
   www.scarestreet.com/terrorintheshadows
6. Monster Collection
   www.scarestreet.com/monster

And experience the full-length novels (150 – 210 pages):
### Ron Ripley (Ghost Stories)
7. Sherman's Library Trilogy (FREE via mailing list signup)
   www.scarestreet.com

8. The Boylan House Trilogy
www.scarestreet.com/boylantri
9. The Blood Contract Trilogy
www.scarestreet.com/bloodtri
10. The Enfield Horror Trilogy
www.scarestreet.com/enfieldtri

## Moving In Series
11. Moving in Series Box Set Books 1 – 6
www.scarestreet.com/movinginboxfull
12. Moving In Series Box Set Books 1 – 3
www.scarestreet.com/movinginbox123
13. Moving In (Book 1)
www.scarestreet.com/movingin
14. The Dunewalkers (Book 2)
www.scarestreet.com/dunewalkers
15. Middlebury Sanitarium (Book 3)
www.scarestreet.com/middlebury
16. Moving In Series Box Set Books 4 – 6
www.scarestreet.com/movinginbox456
17. The First Church (Book 4)
www.scarestreet.com/firstchurch
18. The Paupers' Crypt (Book 5)
www.scarestreet.com/paupers
19. The Academy (Book 6)
www.scarestreet.com/academy

## Berkley Street Series
20. Berkley Street Series Books 1 – 9
www.scarestreet.com/berkleyfullseries
21. Berkley Street (Book 1)
www.scarestreet.com/berkley
22. The Lighthouse (Book 2)
www.scarestreet.com/lighthouse
23. The Town of Griswold (Book 3)
www.scarestreet.com/griswold
24. Sanford Hospital (Book 4)
www.scarestreet.com/sanford

25. Kurkow Prison (Book 5)
www.scarestreet.com/kurkow
26. Lake Nutaq (Book 6)
www.scarestreet.com/nutaq
27. Slater Mill (Book 7)
www.scarestreet.com/slater
28. Borgin Keep (Book 8)
www.scarestreet.com/borgin
29. Amherst Burial Ground (Book 9)
www.scarestreet.com/amherst

## Hungry Ghosts Street Series
30. Hungry Ghosts (Book 1)
www.scarestreet.com/hungry

## Haunted Collection Series
31. Collecting Death (Book 1)
www.scarestreet.com/collecting
32. Walter's Rifle (Book 2)
www.scarestreet.com/walter
33. Blood in the Mirror (Book 3)
www.scarestreet.com/bloodmirror
34. Hank's Radio (Book 4)
www.scarestreet.com/hanksradio
35. The Burning Girl (Book 5)
www.scarestreet.com/theburninggirl
36. Knife in the Dark (Book 6)
www.scarestreet.com/knife
37. Last Breath (Book 7)
www.scarestreet.com/lastbreath
38. Ticket to Death (Book 8)
www.scarestreet.com/tickettodeath
39. Death Rattle (Book 9)
www.scarestreet.com/deathrattle

## Haunted Village Series
40. Worthe's Village (Book 1)
www.scarestreet.com/worthesvillage

41. Hell's Hammer (Book 2)
   www.scarestreet.com/hellshammer
42. Butcher's Hands (Book 3)
   http://scarestreet.com/butchershands
43. Soul Harvest (Book 4)
   http://scarestreet.com/soulharvest

## Victor Dark (Supernatural Suspense)
44. Uninvited Guests Trilogy
   www.scarestreet.com/uninvitedtri
45. Listen To Me Speak Trilogy
   www.scarestreet.com/listentri

## A.I. Nasser (Supernatural Suspense)
46. Listen to Me Now
   www.scarestreet.com/listentomenow

## Slaughter Series
47. Slaughter Series Books 1 – 3 Bonus Edition
   www.scarestreet.com/slaughterseries
48. Children To The Slaughter (Book 1)
   www.scarestreet.com/children
49. Shadow's Embrace (Book 2)
   www.scarestreet.com/shadows
50. Copper's Keeper (Book 3)
   www.scarestreet.com/coppers

## Sin Series
51. Kurtain Motel (Book 1)
   www.scarestreet.com/kurtain
52. Refuge (Book 2)
   www.scarestreet.com/refuge
53. Purgatory (Book 3)
   www.scarestreet.com/purgatory

## The Carnival Series
54. Blood Carousel (Book 1)
   www.scarestreet.com/bloodcarousel

## Witching Hour Series

## David Longhorn (Supernatural Suspense)
## The Sentinels Series

## Dark Isle Series

## Ouroboros Series

## Curse of Weyrmouth Series

## Nightmare Series

68. Nightmare Series Box Set Books 1 – 3
    http://scarestreet.com/nightmarebox
69. Nightmare Abbey (Book 1)
    www.scarestreet.com/abbey
70. Nightmare Valley (Book 2)
    www.scarestreet.com/nightmarevalley
71. Nightmare Revelation (Book 3)
    www.scarestreet.com/revelation
72. Nightmare Resurrection (Book 4)
    www.scarestreeet.com/resurrection
73. Nightmare Spawn (Book 5)
    www.scarestreeet.com/spawn
74. Nightmare Rising (Book 6)
    www.scarestreet.com/rising

## Mephisto Club Series

75. Dark Waters (Book 1)
    www.scarestreet.com/darkwaters
76. Spider Maze (Book 2)
    www.scarestreet.com/spidermaze
77. Ghost Machine (Book 3)
    www.scarestreet.com/ghostmachine

## Sara Clancy (Supernatural Suspense)
## Dark Legacy Series

78. Black Bayou (Book 1)
    www.scarestreet.com/bayou
79. Haunted Waterways (Book 2)
    www.scarestreet.com/waterways
80. Demon's Tide (Book 3)
    www.scarestreet.com/demonstide

## Banshee Series

81. Midnight Screams (Book 1)
    www.scarestreet.com/midnight
82. Whispering Graves (Book 2)
    www.scarestreet.com/whispering

83. Shattered Dreams (Book 3)
www.scarestreet.com/shattered
84. Rotting Souls (Book 4)
www.scarestreet.com/rottingsouls

## Black Eyed Children Series
85. Black Eyed Children (Book 1)
www.scarestreet.com/blackeyed
86. Devil's Rise (Book 2)
www.scarestreet.com/rise
87. The Third Knock (Book 3)
www.scarestreet.com/thirdknock

## Demonic Games Series
88. Demonic Games (Book 1)
www.scarestreet.com/nesting
89. Buried (Book 2)
www.scarestreet.com/buried
90. Captive (Book 3)
www.scarestreet.com/captive

## Wrath and Vengeance Series
91. Pound of Flesh (Book 1)
www.scarestreet.com/flesh
92. Devil's Playground (Book 2)
www.scarestreet.com/playground
93. Scorched Earth (Book 3)
www.scarestreet.com/scorched

## The Plague Series
94. Ring of Roses (Book 1)
www.scarestreet.com/ringofroses
95. Pocket of Posies (Book 2)
www.scarestreet.com/posies
96. Ashes to Ashes (Book 3)
www.scarestreet.com/ashes

**Chelsey Dagner (Supernatural Suspense)**
**<u>Ghost Mirror Series</u>**
  97. Ghost Mirror (Book 1)
      <u>www.scarestreet.com/ghostmirror</u>
  98. Gatekeeper (Book 2)
      <u>www.scarestreet.com/gatekeeper</u>
  99. Grave Games (Book 3)
      <u>www.scarestreet.com/gravegames</u>


**See you in the shadows,**
**Team Scare Street**

Made in the USA
Middletown, DE
04 June 2020

96496651R00096